The Plant That Ate Dirty Socks

The Plant That Ate Dirty Socks

Nancy McArthur

HARCOURT BRACE & COMPANY

Orlando   Atlanta   Austin   Boston   San Francisco   Chicago   Dallas   New York

Toronto   London

This edition is published by special arrangement with Avon Books.

Grateful acknowledgment is made to Avon Books for permission to reprint *The Plant That Ate Dirty Socks* by Nancy McArthur. Copyright © 1988 by Nancy McArthur.

Printed in the United States of America

ISBN 0-15-305215-5

1 2 3 4 5 6 7 8 9 10   060   97 96 95 94

To my nephews and literary consultants,
Michael R. McArthur and Chad P. McArthur,
my sister-in-law Barbara Berg McArthur,
and my very neat sister and brother,
Susan Lee McArthur and John Palmer McArthur

Chapter 1

Michael was the world's messiest kid. His brother Norman, three years younger, was a neatness nut.

This would not have been such a big problem except that they shared the same room.

Norman's side looked like a picture in a magazine.

Michael's side looked like a junk heap.

There were clothes crumpled on the floor, socks and comic books under the bed, model kits with pieces scattered all over, baseball cards, rocks, bird feathers, pine cones, and heaps of books and papers. And that was just the top layer.

When Norman was supposed to make his bed, he just did it. When Michael was forced to make his bed, first he had to find it.

Mom kept saying about forty-two times a week, "Pick that up. Put this away. Throw that out."

Dad kept saying, "Where does all this stuff come from? Is it multiplying at night when we're asleep?"

1

Norman kept complaining, "Your junk is oozing across the middle into my side of the room!"

"I'm going to build a wall," he yelled, "to defend myself from all that messiness!"

Michael yelled back, "I'll build a wall so I won't have to look at all that neatness!"

"No walls," said Mom. "How about drawing a line?"

They measured to find the exact middle. Then they made the line with tape right across the rug.

Norman had fun kicking Michael's things back across the line if they were sticking over even just a tiny bit.

When Michael had any clear space, he told Norman, "Your neatness is oozing over on my side! Ugh!"

Then he would strew more stuff around than before. Even a touch of neatness would look like giving in.

He daydreamed about inventing a robot that would make his bed, clean up, and take Norman on a spaceship to another planet.

Then he could amaze everybody by entering the robot in the school science fair. This was the first year his grade could enter. It was a long way off, but his friends were already getting good project ideas.

One of these days he was going to look through his junk to find something to make a really different project. In the meantime the piles of stuff kept getting higher.

He usually got his clothes off the floor and into the wash so he would have something to wear. But his dirty socks seemed to keep escaping. They got under the bed, under a book, under anything big enough for a balled-up sock to hide under.

Mom said, "We're not buying any more until your feet get too big for the ones you've got. Keep digging until you find those missing socks."

At laundry time Michael would go on a sock hunt.

But he never seemed to find them all. Sometimes he found things that had been buried for months.

"Help!" yelled Norman. "This room is sinking under all this junk!"

Michael put a few things in the wastebasket to shut him up. He could get them back out later.

"Someday," Norman warned, "I'm going to throw all this out when you're not home. Then I won't tell you where I threw it so you can't get it back."

"Don't you dare," said Michael.

"Maybe I'll just throw away one thing at a time. You'll never notice what's gone."

Norman was a big pain in the neck, but once in a while Michael made a deal with him. If he wanted something from Norman, he would trade him some good junk he didn't want anymore. If Norman wanted something from him, Michael would get him to help clean up, since he was so good at it.

"See? It's easy," Norman would say.

"Not for me," said Michael. "It's not one of my many talents."

Michael hated to throw anything away.

Dad asked why he was keeping some mysterious pieces of metal and three dead batteries. He explained, "I might be able to make something out of those."

Mom told him to throw out the rocks and empty pop cans. He explained, "Those are two of my collections."

Norman protested about Muncho Cruncho cereal box tops all over the place. Michael explained, "As soon as I save up twenty-five of them, I'm sending in for a free plastic race car kit."

Michael was always sending away for things. It usually took so long for them to come in the mail that when they did arrive it was a nice surprise.

One day he got a small package with two dried beans in it. The leaflet with them said: "Here are the Amazing Beans you ordered. For best results follow directions carefully."

There was no clue about what kind of plants these beans would grow to be. Michael could not remember what he had sent for.

He planted one of the seeds in a big flower pot and put it on his side of the sunny windowsill between the beds. The leaflet got lost, so he dumped some water in the pot and hoped that was the right amount.

Norman said, "Whatever the plant turns out to be, it better not grow big and ooze all over my side of the window!"

To shut him up, Michael gave him the other bean to grow.

Norman watered his carefully every morning with his Super Splasher Water Blaster, a bigger than regular water pistol.

Michael warned, "Yours better not ooze over on my side. If it does, my plant will strangle your plant."

"Just what we needed," said Mom, "dueling plants."

Every morning and afternoon after school, they looked to see if anything was happening with the Amazing Beans. Nothing.

Then in Norman's pot a tiny green dot appeared. "My plant is growing faster than your plant," boasted Norman.

"Oh, no," said Dad. "Now they're having a plant race."

Two days later Michael saw a pale green speck in his pot. "Come on, plant," he said, "let's go!"

The next morning it had grown an inch. After school it was four inches high.

"Amazing," he said. "Now I know how that story about Jack and the beanstalk got started."

Norman's plant started catching up.

Michael saw a TV commercial that said plants grow bigger if you feed them with plant food. He asked his mother if they had any.

"Look way back in the cupboard under the sink," she answered. "If there's any left, it's in a green bottle."

He found a half-full green bottle without a label. He poured it on his plant and threw the bottle away.

Mom called, "Be sure to give Norman half the plant food."

"But I already used it all."

"Oh, I hope it won't hurt your plant. You're only supposed to use a tiny bit and mix it with water. I'll buy another bottle so Norman can feed his, too."

As the plants grew higher, so did the piles of Michael's stuff. His parents told him they were all going to a space movie Saturday. If he didn't clean up by then, he could not go.

He kept putting off getting started. So he didn't get it done.

When his parents and Norman were going out the door to the movie, Mom said, "You have to clean all that up by the time we get back or else."

"Or else what?" asked Michael.

"I don't know, but by the time we get back I'll think of something."

"You've got two hours," said Dad, "so hurry up."

Two hours later, Michael was still dawdling along when Mom called up from a pizza place. "I've thought of an 'or else'. If you're done cleaning up, we'll bring home a pizza. If not, we'll eat it here."

For pizza Michael would do almost anything. "Bring it home," he said. "I'll be done when you get here."

When they arrived, all the junk was gone.

Mom said, "You did a wonderful job."

Dad said, "Nice work, son. What did you do with all that stuff?"

"He must have hired a trash truck," said Norman, peering suspiciously under all the furniture. "Where's my fishing hat?"

"You're wearing it," said Michael.

"No, this is my baseball cap. My fishing hat is the green one. What did you do with it?"

"I haven't seen it. Where did you leave it?"

"It must be in the closet," said Norman.

"No," said Michael. "I wouldn't look in there."

"Why not? What's in there you don't want me to see?"

"Norman, don't open that door!"

"Why not?"

"Uh . . . there's a monster in there."

"Ha!" said Norman, grabbing the doorknob. "Get out of my way!"

"You won't like it," warned Michael.

"This closet's half mine, so if there's a monster in here, it better be on your side," said Norman.

He yanked the door open.

"Aha!" he exclaimed as stacks of Michael's stuff fell out in an avalanche all over him.

"Norman, are you all right?" Michael asked the pile of stuff. Two eyes and a baseball cap, slightly dented, were sticking out of it.

"Gurfiss. Gurfiss," said Norman.

"What?" Michael cleared the stuff away from Norman's mouth.

"I'll get you for this," Norman was saying.

"I told you not to open the door." Michael dug him out. "You made all this fall out of the closet, so now you have to help me clean it up."

"No way!" screeched Norman. He stomped out of the room.

Michael started over. He stacked half the stuff in shorter piles in his half of the closet. He crammed the rest under his bed. He even put a few things in the wastebasket.

By the time he got his share of the pizza, it was cold.

"Pizza is good for you," said Dad, "even when it's cold."

"Maybe it's good for plants, too," Michael thought. So he stuck some tiny pieces of pizza into the dirt around his plant.

Chapter 2

Both plants were growing fast. The sprouts turned into strange vines and began crawling up the window.

As the days passed, little leaves spread out into long pointed shapes. Then they curled up like dark green ice cream cones.

Norman said, "These plants look weird."

"You're right about something for once," Michael agreed.

Michael's friend Jason, who lived on the other side of town, had his mother drop him off one Saturday to see the plants. "You're right," he said. "These ARE weird."

Norman was using the bottled plant food, measuring carefully.

Michael sloshed some of that on his plant once in a while. He also slipped it a little dessert—a dab of peanut butter, chocolate chip cookie crumbs, a spoonful of pumpkin pie, and bits of Muncho Cruncho.

His vines got thicker than Norman's. Were they getting fat from all the goodies? He switched to bits of vegetables to see what would happen.

"Can I have a little broccoli, please?" he asked at dinner.

"Why this sudden urge for broccoli?" said Mom, passing it to him. "I usually have to tell you to eat it or else."

"I want to feed some to my plant."

"Aha!" said Norman. "No fair feeding your plant extra stuff!"

"I'm just experimenting."

Dad said, "Those plants are getting too big too fast. If they keep on like this, they'll fill up the whole room. So no more feeding them plant food. Not even broccoli. Just sun and water."

"But that will wreck my experiment," protested Michael.

"No, you've seen how it grows with feeding. Now see how it grows without it."

"But what if it collapses from no food?"

Dad smiled. "That plant looks as if it can take care of itself."

Mom added, "It looks as if it could take over the whole house. Now eat your broccoli or else."

"Or else what?" asked Michael with his mouth full of broccoli.

"Or else tomorrow we'll have those plants for dinner," joked Mom.

Both plants slowed down. Then Norman's seemed to stop growing while Michael's kept getting bigger.

"Are you sneaking food to yours," asked Norman, "when I'm asleep?"

"No, honest, I'm not," replied Michael. He was puzzled, too.

"Then why is yours still growing when mine isn't?"

"Maybe my messy growing methods work better than your neat ones."

Mom came in with a laundry basket. They handed over their dirty clothes. But Michael could find only five escaped socks.

"There must be more here somewhere," he said.

"They'll turn up," said Mom, "the next time you clean up."

But they didn't. The next time he found only three.

This mystery, he decided, was easy to solve.

"Norman, you're swiping my socks and hiding them when I'm asleep!"

"Nope, honest, I'm not. I wouldn't touch your yukky old socks!"

"OK, you guys," said Mom. "We're all going to look until we find them. Norman, why are you putting on your football helmet?"

"Because I'm going to look in the closet." He yanked the door open.

"Avalanche!" he yelled, but not much fell out. He was only up to his knees in junk. Norman looked disappointed. He high-stepped out of the pile and dived into the back of the closet.

Michael found one sock in his acorn collection box.

Mom found another one in a bulging book called *The Glob That Ate Outer Space.*

"Don't lose my place," said Michael, putting a blue jay feather between the pages where the sock had been.

"Aha!" exclaimed Norman from the closet. A rolled-up sock came flying out and bounced off Michael's head.

"Aha! Aha!" shouted Norman. Two more zoomed through the air and bonked Michael.

11

"Stop throwing socks!" yelled Michael.

"I can't stop throwing them."

"Why not?"

"Because I'm kicking them!" Another sock sailed overhead.

"If you don't stop that," Michael warned, "I'm going to drop-kick your football helmet with you in it."

"No fighting," said Mom. "And no more sock kicking."

Norman came out holding a sock with one hand and his nose with the other.

"Give me that," Mom said. "Now we're missing at least ten more."

They looked into and under everything. No more socks.

"Strange," said Mom, "that there were more in the closet than out here."

"Yeah," said Michael. "Mostly I drop my socks right around here by my bed."

That night when he took off his socks, he put them on top of his acorn box right next to the bed. That way they could not get lost among his junk.

In the morning they were gone.

"OK, Norman, very funny. Where are the socks I put right here last night?"

"I didn't touch your smelly old socks."

"Well, they couldn't walk away by themselves."

"Why not? Socks have feet in them."

"Come on, where did you hide them?"

"Maybe the monster in the closet took them."

"The only monster that's been in that closet is you."

"Honest, I didn't take them. Something very weird is going on."

They looked all over. They even used the magnifying glass from Norman's detective kit to search for clues.

But the socks had disappeared without a trace.

At bedtime Michael told Norman, "We're going to solve this mystery tonight."

"Good, I love to detect," said Norman.

Michael dug around in his stuff and found some black string he had known would come in handy some day.

He took off his socks, tied the strings to them, and put them where the others had vanished. Then he got into bed, lay there with his arms straight out, and told Norman to tie the strings to his wrists.

Norman got his Super Splasher Water Blaster and favorite disguise from his detective kit and climbed into bed.

"You don't need a disguise in the dark," said Michael.

"I always detect better when I'm wearing one," replied Norman. He turned out the light and put on his disguise.

"Ready?" asked Michael.

"Ready," said Norman.

They had left the door ajar so a little light came in from the hall. They could barely see the white socks on the floor.

They lay there in the dark waiting. Nothing happened. They waited some more. Norman was lying on his side staring at the socks.

Suddenly one moved!

"It's moving!" he shouted and began squirting wildly with his Water Blaster.

"Oh, no!" yelled Michael.

"I saw it!" Norman insisted excitedly. "It was creeping fast across the floor! Then it jumped up in the air and fell down! There it goes again!" he yelled, bouncing up and down on his bed and squirting more water in every direction.

"No," said Michael. "My nose started to itch. I forgot and reached up to scratch it."

Their parents ran in and turned on the light.

There was Michael with strings and socks dangling. Water was dripping off his hair and the end of his nose.

Norman was waving a giant water pistol and wearing glasses with an attached rubber nose and moustache.

Water was dripping off the plants, soaking into the rug and beds, and running down the walls.

"I know," said Mom, "that there has to be a logical explanation for all this, but it better be a good one, or else."

As they wiped up with towels, Michael explained.

Mom took the socks for safekeeping. Norman refilled his Water Blaster, but Dad took it away from him.

"But I need that," wailed Norman, "to water my plant!"

"No," said Dad. "Everything in this room has been watered enough already. I'll keep it next to my bed so there won't be any more midnight underwater adventures in here."

Since the beds were damp, Michael and Norman had to spend the rest of the night on the living room couch, one at each end with their feet kicking each other in the middle.

As they were falling asleep, Michael whispered, "Tomorrow I'll think of a new master plan."

Chapter 3

But the next day he decided to try his original master plan once more. It might have worked if his nose hadn't itched.

"But what if your nose itches again?" asked Norman.

"I'm only going to use one sock so I'll have one hand to scratch."

Norman said, "I don't have my Water Blaster, so I'll use my bow and rubber suction cup arrows."

"Your aim with that," said Michael, "would be worse than the water pistol. We'd end up with rubber arrows stuck all over me and the ceiling."

"Then I'll just wear a disguise so if something is stealing your socks I can scare it off. My robot helmet looks pretty scary. See, if something sneaks in here, it'll expect to see kids in our beds. Not a robot. You should wear a disguise, too. Then it will get really scared."

Michael thought Norman's idea was dumb but wouldn't

hurt. He dug around in his stacks and pulled out a rubber gorilla head.

"Where did you get that?" asked Norman, his eyes lighting up.

"I traded Jason Greensmith a lot of stuff for it. He terrified everybody in his neighborhood with it last Halloween."

"It doesn't look very scary," said Norman.

"It does when you have it on," replied Michael.

"Oh, good! Can I wear it? Please!"

Michael could see this would be the perfect thing to make a deal with the next time he wanted something big from Norman.

"No, maybe we can make a deal later," he said. "I'm going to wear it tonight. You get your robot helmet."

After they went to bed they whispered back and forth in the dark until they heard their parents close their bedroom door.

Then they got their flashlights from under the blankets where they had hidden them. Norman tied the string to Michael's wrist. Michael tied the other end to the sock. Then they turned off the flashlights, got back into bed, and put on their disguises.

"Ready?" asked Michael.

"Ready," said Norman.

They waited a long time.

Suddenly Norman whispered, "If your nose itches, remember don't use the wrong hand."

"OK, OK."

They waited some more.

Norman whispered, "How will you scratch your nose with that mask on?"

"My nose is probably not going to itch. It hardly ever does."

"But what if it does?"

"The mask has big holes under the nose to breathe. I can scratch through there."

"Be sure not to use the wrong hand."

"Will you stop worrying about my nose!"

"I just want to be sure after what happened the last time."

"Norman, if we're going to find out what makes these socks disappear, we have to keep quiet. It only happens when we're asleep, so we have to pretend we are."

Norman was quiet for a long time. Nothing happened. Then he whispered, "I hope it's a raccoon."

"Why?"

"I like raccoons."

"Norman, stop it!"

"OK, OK."

Then Michael whispered, "Now don't get excited. I'm just going to scratch my nose."

"I knew this would happen," said Norman. "Are you using the wrong hand?"

"No!"

It was getting late. Lying there in the dark, pretending to be asleep, they could not stay awake.

Michael woke suddenly. Something was tugging on the string!

He whispered, "It's moving," to Norman and switched on his flashlight.

He saw something green curling around the white sock. A long vine from his plant was dragging it along the floor.

He yelled at Norman to wake up.

"Smurg," mumbled Norman, still completely konked out.

The vine lifted the sock up to one of the big curled leaves. The ice cream cone shape slowly began sucking it in.

"Schlurrrrrp," said the plant as the sock disappeared.

"Wake up!" shouted Michael as he cut the string from his wrist.

Norman, who had fallen asleep holding his flashlight, turned it on.

Seeing a gorilla looming up in the dark, he gave a bloodcurdling "EEEEEEK," leaped from his bed, and zoomed out the door.

His parents, awakened by the horrible noises, were getting out of bed to come to the rescue. Suddenly they saw a ghostly robot hurtle into their room.

Dad, still half-asleep, grabbed Norman's Super Splasher Water Blaster from the bedside table. He let the robot have it right in the snoot.

At the first cold wet squirt, Norman ducked and disappeared.

Michael, running in right behind him, got the rest of the water.

Mom turned on the light. A short gorilla in wet pajamas stood at the end of the bed.

"You're not going to believe this," he said, "but my plant just ate my sock."

"You're right," said the gorilla's mother. "I don't believe any of this."

Dad looked around. "I saw something in the dark that looked like a robot. Where's Norman?"

"Down here," said a familiar voice from under the bed. "I thought a gorilla was after me."

Mom grabbed his feet and pulled him out.

"Remember," she asked, "when nights used to be

normal around here? When everybody went to bed and just stayed there? What's next? Frankenstein and Wolfman?''

"My friend Bob's got a good Frankenstein mask I could borrow," Norman suggested helpfully.

"No way," said Dad. "Now Michael, what about this dream you had about your plant?"

"It wasn't a dream. I woke up and saw it suck up my sock!"

Dad said soothingly, "Everybody has amazing dreams once in a while that seem real."

Michael turned to Norman. "You woke up while it was happening. Tell Dad what you saw."

"All I saw was a gorilla coming at me in the dark. But I'm not going back in there. That plant might get me!" He clutched his throat and made a horrible noise.

"Nothing is going to get you," said Mom. "I think you've both been reading too many books like *The Glob That Ate Outer Space*. Let's find you some dry pajamas. Then we'll check out that plant. You'll see it was only a dream and there's nothing to be afraid of."

Michael explained, "It won't come after us. It only eats socks."

Dad led the way to the boys' room and turned on the light.

"See?" said Mom. "Your plant is just sitting there doing nothing as usual."

Michael walked up to it. "But I saw it eat the sock." He picked a black string off the floor. "This was tied to the sock. Here's the end I cut. The other end looks sort of chewed."

His parents looked closely.

"There must be some logical explanation for this," said Mom, "but I have no idea what it is."

19

Michael replied, "The logical explanation is that the plant ate my sock. Especially since I saw it."

"There is a Venus-flytrap plant that eats insects," said Dad, "but this is ridiculous."

"This must be a Sock Trap plant," said Norman.

"The way it's been growing," said Mom, "and with all the socks we're missing, I wouldn't be surprised."

"I'll prove it to you with an experiment," said Michael. He took a pair of socks from his dresser drawer and put one in front of his plant and the other in front of Norman's. He tied black string around them and fastened the other ends to the bedposts.

"Now Norman and I will sleep on the couch. We'll lock this door. In the morning you'll see what happened."

He turned out the lights, locked the door, and gave the key to Mom.

A moment after the door closed, Michael's plant rustled its leaves as if a little breeze were passing by. Then it made a funny noise that sounded like a contented burp after a good meal.

Chapter 4

Michael woke up early and awakened everyone else. Mom handed over the key. Michael slowly opened the door.

They stared in amazement.

The sock in front of Michael's plant was still there. But the one in front of Norman's had vanished!

Michael was baffled.

Norman was upset. "Your plant reached over on my side of the room! It's not supposed to do that!"

"I don't think it did," said Michael. He pointed to the string still tied to Norman's bedpost. The other end was hanging from Norman's plant.

"My plant wouldn't eat your yukky old dirty socks," Norman protested.

"That's it!" exclaimed Michael. "Those socks weren't dirty. I got them out of the drawer. The ones that disappeared before were dirty. That's the only kind I leave on the floor. So my plant only likes dirty socks. It didn't want a clean one."

"Then why hasn't Norman's eaten clean ones before?" asked Mom.

"There haven't been any clean ones lying around. Norman never leaves anything around for long."

Norman's plant rustled its leaves.

"Where did that breeze come from?" asked Dad.

"There isn't any breeze," said Mom. "None of the windows are open."

The plant burped.

"That was definitely a burp," said Mom.

"Maybe we could teach it to say excuse me," suggested Norman.

"So what we have here," said Mom, "are two plants with finicky appetites. One only eats dirty socks and the other eats clean ones. That's what's going on here?"

Michael said, "That's the logical explanation."

"Don't talk to me about logical," said Mom. "This is wacko."

At breakfast Mom said, "Those plants have to go."

"Go where?" asked Norman.

"In the trash. The city dump. Outer space. Anywhere but in this house."

"No!" protested Michael. "These are great plants! We have to keep them."

"They're creepy," said Mom, "and they eat socks. Do you have any idea how much socks cost?"

"Yeah," added Dad. "Your plant has already caused a severe sock shortage, and now Norman's is starting."

"But these plants are special," said Michael. "And we grew them ourselves from seeds."

Norman whined, "And mine burps. You can't throw it out! I'll never find another one that can do that!"

"Just give them a chance for a little while," pleaded Michael. "You'll see they won't be any trouble."

"What about the socks?" said Mom.

"We won't leave any on the floor, so they can't eat any," said Michael.

"Hmmm," said Mom, stalling while she tried to think up another reason. "What if they get hungry and start munching on something else?"

"They won't," argued Michael. "They only eat socks."

"Then maybe it wouldn't hurt to keep them a while," said Dad. "But if anything goes wrong, out they go."

"All right," agreed Mom, "but those plants better behave."

"Great," said Michael. "Wait till I tell everybody at school. Will they ever be surprised!"

"Yeah," said Norman. "I bet we'll be on TV!"

"Oh, no, you won't," said Dad. "You both have to promise that you won't tell anyone that those plants eat socks."

"But that's the best part!" exclaimed Michael. "It's amazing!"

"I have to tell everybody, too," said Norman.

"Absolutely not," said Dad. "If some kid told you at school today that he has a plant that eats sneakers, what would you think?"

"That he's a liar," said Norman.

"Right," said Dad. "Nobody would believe you. It would be very embarrassing. If you want to keep your plants a little longer, we're not going to get into that."

"But we could bring people home to show them that it's true," said Michael.

"In the middle of the night?" asked Mom. "That's ridiculous. And if word got out, we'd probably wind up on the front page of one of those weird newspapers at the supermarket—right next to a picture of Bigfoot."

"That would be great," said Norman excitedly. "I like Bigfoot!"

"On the other hand," said Mom, "if word got out, surely we'd get offers from scientists to buy the plants and take them away for experiments. That would be a good way to get rid of them."

"No!" shouted Norman. "Not my plant!"

"Listen," said Dad, "I'm due for a promotion I've been working hard for. You know I even gave up some vacations. If people start gossiping about our having plants that eat socks, we'll sound like the biggest weirdos in town."

"True," agreed Mom.

"My boss likes big plants," Dad continued. "He has some in his office. But he is probably not going to be eager to promote somebody with a weirdo reputation. And I don't want you two being called liars at school. So it's better just not to bring this up at all."

"I guess you're right," said Michael glumly.

"If you want to keep those crazy plants," Dad said firmly, "you have to promise not to mention the socks. Talk all you want about the plants, but not about their favorite food. Is it a deal?"

"Deal," agreed Michael.

"Norman?" asked Dad.

He kicked a chair and scowled. "Deal," he said.

"Me, too," said Mom. "My lips are zipped."

They all shook on it.

That night Michael dropped his dirty socks and other clothes on the floor as usual. Then he picked them up and tossed them in the closet where his plant could not get at them. He was sure it would not be interested in munching on any of his other junk.

Chapter 5

Early the next morning Michael heard a burp. He thought he was dreaming and didn't bother to open his eyes.

But then he heard Norman saying softly, "Come on, say excuse me. Excuse me. Excuse me. OK, try it one word at a time. Ex, ex, ex."

Michael opened his eyes. Norman was talking to his plant.

"What are you doing?"

"If I can teach it to say excuse me, it'll be the only plant in the world that can burp and talk, too. Then Mom and Dad will have to let me keep it forever."

"You didn't feed it, did you?"

"Only one clean sock. Just to get it to burp."

"You can't do that! I said we wouldn't let them eat socks. If Mom and Dad find out about this, the plants will be goners."

Norman protested, "But you fed yours."

"I did not!"

"Maybe you didn't mean to," said Norman, pointing, "but your acorn collection is gone."

So was the library book Michael had left the acorn collection on top of the night before. This was serious. It meant he would have to pay for the library book out of his allowance. It also meant that nothing he left lying around was safe any more. He pulled the covers over his head to think about this terrible development.

"Say ex," continued Norman patiently.

When Michael got up to get dressed, he noticed his plant did not look as healthy as usual. It drooped a little, and some leaves were looking a bit yellow around the edges.

"You shouldn't have eaten that library book," Michael told it sternly.

"What's wrong with your plant?" asked Mom. "It looks sick."

Norman blurted out, "It ate Michael's acorns and a library book for breakfast."

"Thanks a lot, blabbermouth!" said Michael.

Mom was upset, to put it mildly. "I told you those plants are trouble. If they'll eat acorns and library books, they'll eat anything!"

"Only one library book," said Michael. "And don't worry, I'm going to pay for it."

Norman exclaimed, "I wish your plant would eat all your junk so we'd have a clean room all the time!"

Michael argued, "It only ate that stuff because it didn't have socks."

"It looks like it's going to throw up," said Norman helpfully. "If a plant eats acorns, will it turn into an oak tree?"

Mom said, "We're getting rid of these crazy plants!"

"No!" screeched Norman. "Mine didn't do anything wrong!"

Michael thought fast. He really wanted to keep his plant. But was it worth the supreme sacrifice? He decided yes.

He asked Mom, "What if I stop leaving anything lying around? Then my plant couldn't eat anything."

Her eyes lit up. "You mean you'd clean up your side of the room without being forced to? And keep it that way? I'd never have to nag you about it? No more messiness?"

Michael swallowed hard. He thought he could handle it for a little while at least. "Yes," he said.

"That's a great idea!" Mom exclaimed. "It's a deal."

Michael started putting his stuff away fast.

Dad brought him some cardboard boxes. Michael marked them Nature Stuff, Collections, Good Junk, and Best Junk.

Mom marked another one Throw Out or Give Away.

He sat in the midst of his junk, picking up one thing at a time and deciding what box to put it in. The piles were quickly getting smaller.

"It looks like my neatness is finally oozing over on your side," said Norman.

"Ugh," said Michael. "Stacking those boxes up would make a good wall."

Norman started jumping over them. "Up, up and away! I leap tall boxes at a single bound!" His foot caught on top of the bulging Best Junk box. He crashed into the Throw Out or Give Away one, which was almost empty.

"The perfect place," said Michael. "Are you all right?"

"Yeah," replied Norman, sliding down so only his feet stuck out. "You're throwing this away? He held up

27

a yellow and blue plastic race car with one wheel missing. "Can I have this?"

"OK."

Mom walked in and saw Norman's feet sticking out of the Throw Out or Give Away box. "I wanted you to clean up, Michael, but this is going too far."

Soon everything was off the floor and into the boxes, drawers, and closet.

Mom walked all around Michael's side of the room where no one had been able to walk before without climbing, slipping, and stumbling. "This is wonderful!" she exclaimed. "Who would have thought these big ugly plants would turn out to be a blessing in disguise!"

"Don't call my plant ugly!" said Norman. "You'll hurt its feelings."

Mom smiled. "I wouldn't want to do that," she said, "not after the way these plants have solved the messiness problem." On her way out the door she turned and said, "Thanks, plants. Keep up the good work."

Michael would never admit it, but he found that neatness was turning out to be pretty good. Now when he wanted to find something, he knew where it was right away. No more digging. No more lost things.

Best of all, Norman was going crazy because he had nothing to complain about.

He did make a nuisance of himself by bragging about how his neatness had taken over, but Michael ignored that.

To keep his plant healthy now that it had no socks to eat, Michael decided to try putting bits of food into the dirt again. He tucked in a little of everything, from vegetables and fruits to cookie crumbs.

But the plant didn't seem to thrive the way it had on socks. It was still bigger than Norman's plant, but it didn't seem to be growing much. He started measuring it and found that for a couple of weeks it didn't grow at all.

"Give it some broccoli," advised Mom.

Michael tried that. But the plant just stood there, limp and tired-looking. Its shade of green seemed much paler. Norman's looked even worse.

"Do something," demanded Norman.

"There's only one thing we know will work," said Michael.

Norman ran to close the bedroom door. "Socks?" he whispered.

"Tonight we'll sneak them a couple," Michael whispered back.

Both plants looked better the next morning. The boys figured a couple of socks would hold them for a few days.

But no. After two more nights without a socks snack, both plants were looking bad again.

"We can keep this up for a little while," said Norman, "but sooner or later Mom's going to notice socks are disappearing."

Michael decided there must be some way to talk Mom into letting them feed the plants socks. After all, she really seemed to like the plants now because they were the cause of all this neatness.

Next morning when he was putting on new socks, he looked at the price tag. Then he got a pencil and multiplied the price by seven.

"Did you think of something?" asked Norman hopefully.

"I'm figuring what it would cost to feed our plants one sock a night each for a week. It's more than both our allowances put together. But what if they could get along on less than a whole sock a night?"

Norman asked, "Like half a sock a night would cost only half as much?"

"Right. That might work. Or we could start with a fourth, and if that doesn't work, then we could try a half. Now I just have to find out how much cat and dog food costs."

"My plant's not going to go for that," said Norman. "Unless I teach it to say woof-woof or meow."

"That's not what I have in mind," said Michael mysteriously as he went to the phone.

He called Kevin Blackstone, who had a cat. He asked him to bring a can of cat food to the phone and read the price. Then he called Chad Palmer, who had a dog.

At school he took all his numbers to Kimberly Offenberg, the class math whiz. He asked her to help him solve the problem of comparing the costs of feeding two pets three different kinds of foods in different amounts. He called them Brands X,Y, and Z, like a television commercial.

"That's easy," said Kimberly. "One-fourth of a can of Brand Z is definitely the cheapest."

Michael smiled. Brand Z was socks.

After school he hurried home to explain the urgent need for socks to Mom and persuade her with the numbers.

"See? One-fourth of a sock a night would cost even less than feeding a cat or dog. Our plants are the cheapest kind of pet. They don't make a mess or any noise. You don't have to walk them. And they make sure I keep our room clean. Isn't that worth a few socks? And it would only cost a little of our allowances to pay for them.''

"Wait a minute!" yowled Norman. "Not my allowance!"

"How much is it worth to you to keep your plant alive?" asked Michael.

That shut him up.

"And maybe Mom will be willing to chip in to keep our room staying neat. Right, Mom?" Michael gave her his most winning smile.

"Hmmm," replied Mom.

Michael pressed on. "This is a good deal for everybody," he argued. "We get our plants to stay alive and well, and you get neatness that lasts. OK?"

"I certainly don't want to give up the neatness," said Mom. "A little extra money for socks would probably be worth it. I could buy them at that discount store, Save-A-Lot. They have very cheap prices on everything."

"But cheap socks might make my plant throw up," whined Norman.

Michael kicked him under the kitchen table, and he shut up.

The nightly socks snacks quickly got both plants looking healthy again and growing. Michael kept on putting bits of food into his plant's pot so his would still grow better than Norman's.

Early one morning, when Michael was still mostly asleep, he heard a contented burp.

Then he heard another one, followed by an "Ex" in a funny voice he had never heard before. "Did you hear?" screeched Norman excitedly.

"Yes," said Michael. "It's amazing. But you'd probably better not mention this to Mom and Dad."

Michael snuggled happily under the covers. As he drifted back to sleep he heard Norman talking in his own voice. "Come on, say meow. Try it. Me, me, me, me. Ow, ow, ow, ow."

There was no reply from the plant.

Chapter 6

Norman kept trying for days.

Michael complained, "I'm sick of you meowing at that plant! It's not a cat!"

"It's my pet," said Norman.

"Then why don't you put a flea collar on it and call it Spot?"

"I'm naming it Fluffy," he replied.

Norman was driving Michael batty.

He said "Good morning" and "Good night" to his plant. He called out, "Hi, Fluffy" when he came in and "Goodbye, Fluffy," when he went out.

Fluffy just stood there.

Norman patted its leaves. He even read it a comic book. When he got home from school, Mom asked, "How did things go today?"

"Fine," said Norman.

"Tell me about it," she said. But Norman was already running off to tell Fluffy.

He also sang to his plant. His favorite was "Camptown Races." He especially liked the "doo-dah-doo-dah" and "oh-doo-dah-day" parts, which he sang at the top of his lungs.

"Keep your noise on your side of the room," snarled Michael.

"I can't do that," said Norman, smiling.

"You can if you shut up completely."

Quiet lasted only a few minutes. Then Norman started howling again, "DOO-DAH-DOO-DAH!"

Michael threw a pillow at him and missed.

When Jason came over one day after school, he was amazed at how much the plants had grown.

"Want to trade for the big one?" he asked Michael. "I just went to a garage sale and got a lot of good stuff to swap. I'll make you a good deal for it."

"Thanks, but no," replied Michael. "I want to keep it."

Jason looked over both plants carefully. "These are so weird they're great. Did you use some special kind of plant food to get them to grow this big or what?"

"Uh . . . well . . . just the kind of stuff everybody has around the house, I guess," said Michael. He wanted to change the subject. "But Norman does something different with his plant," he added. "He sings to it."

"Mine loves music," said Norman, bounding in from the hallway where he had obviously been eavesdropping. "I'll show you." He began howling "Camptown Races."

"Good, Norman," said Jason. To Michael he added, "Let's go outside for a while."

Even though he had lost his audience, Norman howled happily on. Fluffy seemed to be enjoying the concert.

Jason asked Michael if he could come over to his house when his mother picked him up and spend the night.

Mom told Michael, "Absolutely not."

"But why?"

"If you go to Jason's to spend the night, then we'll have to return the invitation and have him spend the night here."

"Great," said Michael. "You always said I could have a friend sleep over someday if I ever got my room cleaned up."

Mom yanked him into the kitchen, closed the door, and lowered her voice to a whisper. "We can't have anyone stay overnight here while those plants are eating you-know-what."

"But," Michael started to protest.

"We'll have to continue this argument later," said Mom. "Norman's singing has given me a headache."

Michael gave up for the moment, but he was certain he could figure out some way to make sure Jason could not possibly see the plants eating socks in the middle of the night.

Everything was going fine with the plants, but Mom was having a problem buying socks. At the Save-A-Lot Discount Store she tried to go to a different checkout clerk each time, but they all noticed she was buying an awful lot of socks.

"You're our best socks customer," one remarked.

"What are your kids doing with all these socks?" joked another. "They must be eating them."

35

Dad suggested she go to different stores. "But Save-A-Lot has the very cheapest socks," she explained.

"Then next time I'll go," he said.

The third time he went, a clerk asked, "Are you by any chance married to a dark-haired lady who buys a lot of socks? We all wondered about her because we haven't seen her lately."

"She's fine," said Dad. "We take turns shopping."

"Your family sure does use a lot of socks," said the clerk. "Your kids must have more than two feet apiece."

When Dad got home, he told Michael it was his turn next time.

Michael didn't argue. He didn't want to give his parents any excuse to change their minds about the plants.

So next time Michael went in while Mom waited in the car.

The checkout clerk looked at the pile of socks and then at Michael. "You look a lot like a man who buys a lot of socks here. Are you by any chance related?"

Back at the car, Michael complained, "I'm not ever going in there again. She wanted to know what we're doing with so many socks."

"What did you tell her?"

"I said our washing machine is broken, so when our socks get dirty we have to throw them away."

Mom groaned.

"But that was all I could think of to say in a hurry."

"Great," said Mom. "Now I'll never be able to show my face in there again."

"You can borrow my gorilla head," he offered.

"Next time," said Mom, "it's Norman's turn."

For the next socks shopping trip Norman wanted to wear a disguise. He put on his fishing hat and Dad's sunglasses.

He also wanted to wear a stick-on moustache from his detective kit, but Mom took it away from him.

They all waited in the car for him.

Norman was gone a long time.

"I'm getting worried," said Mom. "It doesn't take that long to buy socks."

"Maybe one of us better go in after him," said Dad.

"Not me," said Michael. "Maybe with that disguise, he got arrested for impersonating a person."

Just then Norman bounded out with a big package.

"What took you so long?" asked Dad.

"I was picking out some colors of socks, and it was hard to see with sunglasses on. I had to keep peeking out from under them when nobody was looking."

"Why colors?" asked Michael. "Our plants only eat white ones."

"I think Fluffy is getting tired of white all the time."

Mom looked in the bag. "Why brown?" she asked.

"Like chocolate," said Norman.

"And these pink ones are strawberry?"

"Yeah." Norman chuckled delightedly.

She pulled out some white socks with brown stripes.

"Fudge ripple," explained Norman.

The plants had grown so much that they had to be moved into bigger pots. These were hard to turn every few days so that the leaves would get sun evenly on all sides.

As Norman was pushing with all his might, he told Fluffy, "I wish you had wheels."

That gave Michael an idea. He dug through his boxes of junk to find his old skateboard. He had given up skateboarding after a few tries because he kept falling off.

When he put the plant on the skateboard, it kept

37

tipping over. So he traded with Jason for another old board and glued the two sides together. He also wrapped a lot of heavy wire around the boards and the pot to hold everything together solidly.

The stuck-together skateboards made his plant easy to wheel around.

Norman nagged and whined until Mom agreed to get a couple of skateboards for him at garage sales. Michael agreed to help glue and wire them together if Norman would stop bothering him.

"No singing and talking to Fluffy while I'm in the room for two weeks," he demanded.

"Deal," agreed Norman.

So he only talked and sang when Michael was not there. When Michael was in the room, Norman hummed "Camptown Races" loudly instead.

"I didn't promise not to hum," he said with a happy smirk.

Chapter 7

Coming home late from school one day, Michael found a note on the kitchen table: "Back at six. Snacks in refrigerator. Love, Mom. P.S. No humming. No fighting."

Michael called Norman's name. No answer.

He headed for their room. Maybe Norman had not heard him. The door was open. Norman was not there.

Neither was Fluffy.

Michael panicked. Had Fluffy been stolen? Norman would be heartbroken.

But why would burglars take one plant and not Michael's, too? Was anything else gone? For one sinking moment he wondered if Norman was also stolen.

But who else could put up with him for more than five minutes? Especially if he started to sing. Anyone who stole Norman would have brought him back by now.

He calmed down and got Norman's magnifying glass.

There were no clues in the room, but the carpeting in the hall showed faint skateboard tracks. It looked like Fluffy had been rolled out.

He followed the tracks around the corner to the front door. Just outside on the front walk lay another clue—an ice-cream-cone-shaped leaf. Had there been a struggle?

Michael looked up and down the street.

No Fluffy. No burglars. No Norman.

A neighbor, Mrs. Smith, was clipping bushes in her front yard four houses down.

Running over, he called out, "Have you seen anybody go by with a big weird plant—or my brother?"

"Yes, Norman went by a little while ago pushing a very big plant on rollers. When I asked him what he was doing, he said he was taking it for a walk. That Norman! He's so cute, always kidding around!"

"Which way did they go?"

Mrs. Smith pointed toward the end of the street. "Around that corner."

Michael ran on.

Turning the corner, he saw Norman halfway down the block with Fluffy towering over him.

Gathered around were four kids and three grownups. They were touching Fluffy and asking questions: "What kind of plant is this?" "Where can I get one of these?" "How did you get it to grow so big?"

Norman was answering truthfully, "I can't exactly say."

"You'd better come home now," said Michael. He grabbed Fluffy's main stem and pulled. Norman pushed, and they rolled away from the crowd.

"Everybody likes Fluffy," said Norman, "but I didn't think they would ask so many questions."

"You didn't tell about the socks, did you?"

"No, but it was hard not to. If we could tell everybody, we'd be famous. We'd be on TV."

"Forget TV. If we don't keep our deal, it'll be good-bye Fluffy—and my plant, too."

After they turned the corner, the sidewalk slanted slightly downhill, so Fluffy rolled along more easily. They did not have to push or pull, just steer to keep it on the sidewalk.

Michael let go to stop and pick up a blue jay feather. When he caught up, Norman was jogging to keep up with the plant. Michael slowed it down.

They were only six houses from home. In their driveway Dad had come home early and was taking grocery bags out of the car.

Michael noticed a bee following Norman. He warned, "Don't turn around, and don't make any sudden moves."

"Huh?" said Norman.

"Now don't get excited, but there's a bee following you."

Norman held his head still, but the bee flew right towards his face. He let go of Fluffy and ran into the nearest yard.

Michael shoved Fluffy's front wheels onto the edge of the grass and sprinted after Norman.

"Stand still!" he yelled.

Norman stopped. The bee came right up to his nose. He looked at it cross-eyed, but he did not move. Then the bee lost interest in Norman's nose and flew away.

The boys turned back to Fluffy.

But Fluffy was not where Michael had left it. It was rolling away down the sidewalk with its leaves waving in the breeze.

Mrs. Smith looked up from her clipping. She smiled as the huge plant whizzed by.

"Oh, that Norman!" she exclaimed. She called, "Your plant is going for a walk by itself!"

Dad saw the plant zooming down the sidewalk and his sons racing after it.

"Stop that plant!" yelled Michael.

"Fluffy, come back!" shouted Norman.

Dad stepped out on the sidewalk, ready to grab the plant. As it hurtled toward him, he caught hold of a branch.

Fluffy whirled around and tore away from his grasp. But that slowed it enough for Michael to catch up and get a good hold. Norman tackled the pot with both arms.

The boys and Fluffy fell over in a heap on the grass. Dad helped them get untangled.

After he made sure they were not hurt, he got mad.

"What is this plant doing running around loose?" he yelled.

Michael explained. "I thought Fluffy was plantnapped. And maybe Norman, too."

Norman added, "I was just taking Fluffy for a walk. We didn't mean to let him get away. It was the bee's fault."

Dad replied, "When you're both ready to start making sense, let me know. Now get that crazy plant back in the house before anyone else sees it!"

But, of course, the yelling and the sight of a monster plant skateboarding down the block had not gone unnoticed.

Some neighbors were peering out their windows. Others had come outside for a better look. Mrs. Smith was telling them all about it.

Dad smiled and waved at the neighbors, just as if speeding plants were a regular everyday thing.

After they wrestled Fluffy back into the house, Dad warned sternly, "Don't ever take that plant for a walk again!"

Norman said, "I could save up and buy Fluffy a leash."

"No!"

"Handcuffs?" asked Norman hopefully.

"Don't even think it," said Dad.

Norman dropped the subject. He could see Dad was about to start yelling again.

"These plants are getting to be more trouble than they're worth," grumbled Dad.

Michael protested, "Don't blame my plant, too. Mine stayed home and minded its own business."

Dad still looked mad.

At school Jason asked Michael, "Have you thought of something for a science project yet?"

"Not yet. Maybe I'll skip it this year if I can't think of something really great. Are you still going to build a volcano that really works?"

"Yeah, but I haven't figured out how to make it explode or what to use for lava. Maybe you could come over and help me decide what to do. Are you ever going to get permission to sleep over at my house?"

"Pretty soon, I hope. I have to persuade my mom."

"Then hurry up and talk her into it," said Jason. "We'll have a good time staying up late and talking and eating pizza and going through all my junk."

"OK," said Michael. "Then it'll be my turn to have you stay at my house." He added casually, "Do you ever wake up in the middle of the night?"

"Never. My mom and dad always say a marching band could stomp through my room playing full blast and I wouldn't notice. I don't even hear my alarm clock. They have to drag me out of bed by my feet to get me up in the morning."

"You're really a sound sleeper," said Michael, who was happy to hear this.

"Yeah. What did you want to know that for?"

"My mom doesn't like houseguests who wake up easily during the night."

"Why? Does she make a lot of noise at night?"

"No, just having light sleepers in the house would make her nervous."

"Well, I won't make her nervous," Jason assured him. "An elephant stampede wouldn't wake me up."

"We don't have many elephant stampedes," chuckled Michael. "Or marching bands, either. At least not at night."

They both burst out laughing.

The part about the elephant stampede convinced Dad, but Mom still had some doubts.

"We just can't take a chance on Jason seeing the plants eat."

"He'll never know," argued Michael. "He'll be asleep."

Mom protested, "But when I was a kid we stayed up most of the night at sleepovers. Our parents kept getting up and yelling at us to shut up."

"I promise we'll go to sleep long before the plants eat," said Michael.

"Nobody wants to sleep at a sleepover," said Mom.

Michael was ready for that one. "We'll have him over on a Friday night," he explained. "Since that's a school day, we'll all be getting up early that morning, so we won't be able to stay up real late that night. I promise I'll turn out the lights early enough and stop talking to him so he'll have to go to sleep."

"OK," agreed Mom. "But you go to Jason's first just to make sure he really is a sound sleeper. Then we'll be sure we won't be taking any chances."

Chapter 8

So Michael accepted Jason's invitation for a Friday night and took along an alarm clock.

They laughed and ate pizza and went through Jason's junk to pick out some possible stuff for making lava.

Sure enough, since they had gotten up so early that morning, they barely stayed awake until midnight. Jason's mother had to yell at them to shut up only twice.

Late that night, about plant snack time, Michael's alarm went off, waking only Michael. He was delighted to see that Jason did not even twitch.

As soon as Michael got home Saturday, he started making plans for next Friday's sleepover at his house.

Mom said, "You can sleep on the floor and let Jason have your bed."

"What about Norman?" asked Michael.

"What about him? He always goes right to sleep."

"I don't want him in there. We can't talk if he's listening."

"Then make a deal with him. If he lets Jason have his bed for one night, then next weekend he can have Bob over. You can take turns sleeping on the couch. Bob's mother is always joking about what a sound sleeper he is, so it would be safe for him to stay overnight."

Norman hated sleeping on the couch, but all Michael had to do was offer to let him use the gorilla head and he went for it right away.

That night as they were going to sleep, Norman asked, "You're not going to tell Jason about the plants eating socks, are you?"

"Of course not."

"But what if he sees them eating?"

"He won't. He'll be asleep."

"He better be. I don't want anything to happen to Fluffy."

"Nothing is going to happen to Fluffy, or my plant either."

"Don't you love your plant?"

"Sure."

"Then why don't you give it a name? You keep calling it your plant. It's your pet. So it should have a name."

"That's silly."

"But if it doesn't have a name, it must think you don't care about it as much as I care about Fluffy."

"It knows I care about it."

"How can it know if you don't tell it?"

"Norman, go to sleep."

"Good night," mumbled Norman. Then Michael heard him whisper, "Good night, Fluffy. Good night, Michael's plant."

Michael waited a moment. Then he reached out in the

46

the dark and quietly patted a few of his plant's leaves to sort of say good night.

Friday afternoon Mom and Michael changed the sheets on Norman's bed for Jason and put a pillow and blanket on the living room couch.

Norman wheeled Fluffy out next to the couch to spend the night with him there. He suggested to Michael, "Maybe we should put yours out here, too. Then there won't be any chance Jason will wake up and see the plants eating."

"Don't worry, he won't wake up. I already made sure he's a sound sleeper. Besides, he'd wonder why my plant wasn't in my room. He knows that's where I keep it."

"Are you going to tell ghost stories?" asked Norman.

"Maybe."

"Can I listen?"

"No!"

"But if you tell a ghost story, I could listen outside the door and then run in with the gorilla head on. That would really scare Jason. He'd like that."

"That wouldn't scare him. It used to be his gorilla head. Remember?"

"Oh, yeah, I forgot." Norman looked very disappointed.

"You can have some of our pizza," said Michael, "if you eat it somewhere else."

"OK," said Norman. But what could he surprise Jason with? He hated to pass up a good chance to scare somebody.

Of course. His friend Bob's Frankenstein head. That would really surprise Jason—and Michael, too.

He ran all the way over to Bob's to borrow it. He

brought the rubber head home folded up under his sweater and hid it under a couch cushion.

Jason's mother dropped him off after dinner.

"Wow!" he said. "Your plants have gotten a lot bigger. I wish I had one of these. When they grow seeds, can I have some?"

"I don't think these are going to grow seeds," said Michael.

"Norman, do you want to trade for your plant? I've got a lot of good stuff to make a deal with."

"No, it's my pet."

"A pet plant?"

Michael thought Jason would laugh. Instead he said, "That's a good idea."

"You really think so?" asked Michael.

"Sure. My mom won't let me have a cat or dog. She's allergic to every animal I can think of—except snakes and lizards and tarantulas—and she won't let me have one of those, either."

He stroked the leaves on Michael's plant. "A monster one like this would be a great pet. Like a giant weird creature. You could even talk to it and pretend it talks back."

"That's right," said Norman. "I always . . . OW!"

Michael was standing on his foot.

"Why don't you get another kind of big plant?" Michael suggested to Jason.

"Nothing would be as good as this kind," he replied.

When Mom and Dad went to bed, they tucked Norman in on the couch and turned off the lights and TV.

In the quiet he could hear Michael and Jason talking and laughing far off in the bedroom, but he could not hear what they were saying.

48

How could he know when would be a good time to burst in wearing the Frankenstein head unless he could hear what they were talking about?

He took the mask from under the cushion, grabbed his blanket, and crept into the hall.

Just a little light shone from the night-light in the bathroom.

Norman sat down outside the bedroom door to hear if they were telling scary stories yet.

But they were only talking about their friends. Then they started arguing about which teacher at school was the meanest. That was boring.

He pulled the mask over his head to be ready when they changed the subject.

It was getting late. Snuggled in his warm blanket, sitting on the soft carpeting, and leaning against the wall, he decided to close his eyes just for a minute. He could listen with his eyes closed.

Hours later Norman woke up. He had to go to the bathroom. Everything was quiet. Still mostly asleep, he wondered what he was doing in the hall.

He stood up and turned toward the bathroom.

Then he froze.

From the end of the hall in the dim light he saw a Frankenstein monster coming right at him.

He screeched, opened the bedroom door, ran in, and slammed it behind him.

''Monster! Monster!'' he screamed in bloodcurdling tones.

Out of the dark Michael's voice said groggily, ''What? What?'' He turned on the light and saw a short Frankenstein wearing Norman's pajamas.

He was so surprised that he fell right out of bed.

Jason, awakened by the screams, squinted sleepily at both of them.

From the floor Michael asked, "Norman, are you all right?"

"The monster's coming down the hall!" yelled Norman.

Michael was a little more awake now, and things were starting to make sense to him.

"What kind of monster?"

"Frankenstein. Like the mask I got from Bob to scare you."

"Calm down, Norman. You're wearing the mask. I think you saw yourself in the mirror at the end of the hall."

Norman stood behind him as he opened the door. Michael peeked out.

"No monster," he reported.

Norman peeked out. "But I saw it."

Michael pulled him out into the hall. "Look at the mirror," he said.

Norman saw the monster standing next to Michael. He put his hand on his nose and felt a mask. He saw the monster touching its nose, too.

"It's wearing my pajamas," said Norman, "so it must be me. I have to go to the bathroom," he announced and left Michael standing in the hall.

Michael could hardly believe it. After all that, Norman had just gone off to the bathroom as if nothing had happened. The kid was definitely weird.

The other bedroom door opened, and Mom came out.

"You woke me up," she complained. "I want you kids to stop all this noise! Not another peep out of you tonight!"

"It's not my fault," said Michael.

They heard the toilet flush. The bathroom door opened, and a little Frankenstein walked out. Mom screeched.

"It's only Norman," Michael reassured her. "He wanted to scare us."

"He certainly succeeded. Norman, this is not funny!"

"I had to go to the bathroom," Norman replied, as if that explained everything.

Mom said, "Evidently Jason is the only one of you with any common sense. He's still in bed. It must be two or three in the morning."

"Uh-oh," said Michael. He dashed into his room.

Jason was wide awake, staring in stunned amazement at Michael's plant as it ate its nightly meal.

Michael knew he had to do something fast. So he snapped off the light and announced, "We're all having a nightmare together. In the morning we'll really laugh about this. Let's all go back to bed now."

Jason turned the light back on. "Wait a minute. This is not a dream. Your plant is really eating a sock."

"What sock?" asked Norman, trying to be helpful.

"That sock," said Jason. But there was no sock to be seen. The plant had sucked it all in.

"See?" said Norman. "There's no sock there."

"Quit kidding," said Jason. "This is serious. How could you all stand there so calmly while this plant eats a sock? Why aren't you excited about this? You don't even look surprised!"

Then the truth dawned on him.

"You knew all about this before! You've been keeping it a secret! Right?"

Michael did not know what to say.

Mom sent Norman to wake Dad. "You'll have to turn on the light and poke him. He's wearing earplugs so you kids wouldn't keep him awake."

After Norman left the room, Jason whispered, "Why

is he wearing a Frankenstein mask in the middle of the night?''

Michael replied, ''Norman likes disguises at all hours.''

Mom called after Norman, ''Before you wake your father, take off the Frankenstein face!''

Too late. From the other bedroom came a hair-raising screech.

Chapter 9

After Mom got Dad calmed down, the two of them went into the living room to argue in low voices about what to do about Jason's discovery.

Michael's plant rustled its leaves.

Jason asked, "Where did that breeze come from? The window's not open."

"That's not a breeze," said Michael.

The plant burped.

"Did you hear that?" exclaimed Jason excitedly. "It burped! This is great!"

"This is a disaster," Michael told Norman.

"Does yours eat socks, too?" Jason asked Norman. "Does it burp?"

"I promised never to tell," said Norman firmly. "My lips are zipped."

"You can tell me," said Jason. "I won't tell anybody. Besides, I know most of it already."

Norman took off his Frankenstein head and looked at Jason suspiciously.

"We can make a deal," Jason added.

"How?"

"I'll keep quiet about your secret, and you let me have one of the plants!"

"Never!" shouted Norman.

"Jason, you've got to be kidding," said Michael.

"No, I really want one of those plants."

"Guys," called Dad, "come out here and let's talk." The boys sat in a row on the couch.

Dad began, "Jason, you may be wondering about some unusual things you've seen here tonight."

"Your plants eat socks," said Jason. "That's what I saw. It's amazing!"

"Yes, well, er, ah," continued Dad.

"They burp, too," said Jason. "They're great!" He bounced up and down on the couch with enthusiasm, making Michael and Norman bounce, too.

"Well, er, ah, um, Jason, let me put it another way. You're going to have to keep your trap shut about this."

Norman piped up, "Jason tried to blackmail me! He said he'd keep quiet if we'd give him one of our plants!"

Jason protested, "That's not blackmail exactly. Just a deal. I really want a plant like that, and you've got the only two I know of."

"You're not getting Fluffy," said Norman sternly, giving Jason a dirty look. "Not for a million dollars! And you're not getting Stanley either!"

"Who's Stanley?" asked Michael, Mom, Dad, and Jason in a chorus.

"My brother's plant. And you're not getting her!"

"Her?" said everybody.

"That's what I call her," explained Norman. "You

54

can call her whatever you want. Michael hasn't named her yet."

During all this Fluffy had been standing there quietly. Now he rustled his leaves. Then he burped.

"Amazing!" exclaimed Jason.

Then Fluffy said, "Ex."

Jason's mouth fell open. "Who said that?" he asked.

"Me," said Fluffy.

Norman clapped and stamped with delight.

"A talking plant!" screamed Jason. He jumped up to get a better look and bumped into Fluffy.

"Ow," said the plant.

"I'm sorry," Jason apologized. "I didn't mean to hurt you. Are you all right?"

"Me," said Fluffy again.

"Yes, yes?" said Jason anxiously. "Go on. You what?"

"Ow," continued Fluffy.

"You still hurt? Where?"

Fluffy did not reply.

"It's not answering! It must be unconscious!" said Jason frantically. "Somebody do something! Call a plant doctor!"

Norman danced gleefully around the room. Mom and Dad were trying not to laugh out loud.

"OK," said Michael, "we might as well tell Jason the truth about Norman's deep, dark secret powers."

"Huh?" said Norman, Dad, and Mom.

"Unknown to the outside world," Michael continued, "my ordinary-looking brother is in reality a master ventriloquist."

Jason turned to Norman with astonishment. "You throw your voice so it sounds like the plant's talking?"

Norman replied in a strange tone that he hoped sounded like Fluffy: "That's right. I'm a master vantilloquast."

"What?" asked Jason.

Norman tried again. "I mean, vanilla-kissed."

"Nice try," said Jason, "but I don't believe it."

"You believe a plant talks?" asked Michael.

"More than I believe that Norman is a vanilla—a ventilla—throws his voice." Looking exhausted, Jason plopped down in the nearest chair.

"But you know," said Michael soothingly, "that nobody would believe you about a plant eating a sock and another one talking to you."

"True," agreed Jason. "Anybody I told about this would think I wasn't all there upstairs."

"So you promise not to tell anybody?"

"Yeah," said Jason with his eyelids drooping. "But when they get seeds, can I have some?"

"We're hoping there won't be any seeds," said Mom. "Now back to bed. I don't want to hear another peep out of any of you. And that goes for you, too, Fluffy!"

As she and Dad went into their room, Michael heard her say, "Those blasted plants are more trouble than they're worth!" That worried him, but he fell asleep before he had a chance to think about it.

Breakfast was a team effort. Mom supervised and mixed the pancake batter. Dad poured it into circles in the pan, while Michael flipped and shoveled the pancakes onto plates. Jason poured the juice, and Norman set the table.

When no one was looking, Norman poured the whole big bottle of syrup into his Super Splasher Water Blaster. Then he went around squirting at everyone's pancakes and hitting quite a few other things, too.

Mom looked for another bottle of syrup, but there wasn't one. "I don't like it, but I guess we're stuck with the syrup blaster," she concluded.

"Stuck is right," said Dad, wiping syrup drips from his sleeve with a paper napkin that kept tearing apart. Bits stuck to his sleeve and the table.

"This is great," Jason exclaimed and held out his plate. Norman pumped a puddle of goo over his pancakes and hand, too.

"Oops," said Norman. Jason licked his fingers and laughed. "This is a lot better than a plain old bottle," he said.

Michael had to admit to himself that Norman did have a good idea once in a while after all.

When Jason's mother picked him up after breakfast, he told Michael, "My family never does exciting things like yours does. Staying at my house is boring compared to this."

After Jason left, Dad said, "Well, that's it for having anybody stay overnight. We can't do that again until we do something about those plants."

Norman argued, "But I already invited Bob over for next Friday!"

"We'll have to put that off until we figure out what to do. One information leak is bad enough. We're not risking another one."

"No fair," whined Norman. "You promised!"

Michael was getting a sinking feeling in the pit of his stomach. "What do you mean figure out what to do?" he asked.

"The plants are causing problems we didn't think about when we decided to keep them," Dad explained. "Now we know we can't count on anybody sleeping all through the night here. And what do we do when your grandparents come to stay for a whole week? I know if my mother sees one of those plants make a move, she'll call the police first and ask questions later!"

"They won't arrest Fluffy, will they?" asked Norman.

57

"No," said Dad. "Unfortunately not."

"Maybe I should make a disguise for him just in case when Grandma comes," said Norman.

"No," said Mom. "This whole situation is weird enough already."

"But what about my sleepover?" demanded Norman. "You promised!"

"After what happened last night, we can't be sure Bob won't wake up," replied Mom.

"It wasn't my fault," said Norman indignantly. "I had to go to the bathroom! Besides, we could put both our plants in the living room with Michael. Then it won't matter if Bob wakes up. We'd just have to keep him out of the living room. I could build a fence across the door. Or tie Bob's foot to the bedpost, just in case."

"No!" said Mom.

"We could just tell him not to go in the living room," suggested Michael.

"But we'd have to give him a reason," said Dad.

"Let's tell him it's haunted," said Norman.

"No!" said Dad.

"You promised I could have Bob sleep over next Friday," said Norman. He slumped his shoulders and put on his pathetic look that he did so well. "You promised!"

Even Michael felt sorry for him. "I could move the couch across the living room door," he said, "and put the plants next to the same wall. That way Bob couldn't see the plants from the hall if he did wake up. And he couldn't get into the living room without climbing over me. That would wake me up, and I could stop him."

"Well," said Mom, softening.

"That would probably work," said Dad, "and we did promise."

Norman switched on his most winning smile. "And we can have pizza, can't we? Just like you promised?"

"All right," said Mom.

Norman was so happy that he ran off to tell Fluffy, so he did not hear Dad say, "But we still have to do something about those plants."

Now Michael was really worried.

Chapter 10

That night he dreamed that his plant grabbed his grandmother by her socks. That made her so mad that she chopped down both plants with an axe and called the police. They ran in and started singing "Camptown Races." The plants were lying on the floor singing, "Doo-dah-doo-dah." They sounded just like Norman.

Michael woke up. Early morning sunlight was shining through the plant leaves. Norman was howling, "Doo-dah-doo-dah!"

"Ex," said Fluffy.

Michael groaned, "Will you two shut up!" It was going to be a tough day. He went back to sleep.

Jason was so delighted to be in on the secret of the plants that he kept whispering to Michael in school about them. Michael worried about being overheard, so he decided they should use code words—pancakes for socks, Stanley for Michael's plant, and Fluffy for Fluffy.

Then it would not matter if someone heard them whispering about Stanley eating a fudge ripple pancake.

But Pat Jenkins came up behind them suddenly. "Fudge ripple pancakes? That sounds good. Where do you buy those?"

"You can't buy them," said Michael. "You have to make them at home."

"How?" asked Pat.

"Uh . . . you pour some chocolate syrup around in the pancake batter, but don't mix it up. That way you get pancakes with brown stripes."

"I didn't know you were interested in cooking, Michael."

"Only pancakes," said Jason, chuckling.

"What are you laughing about, Jason Greensmith? I'll bet you can't even make regular pancakes."

"I can, too," said Jason. "In the toaster."

"Not frozen ones," said Pat scornfully. "Chocolate striped ones sound delicious. I'm going to try them."

The boys changed the code word to ice cream. But Pat had sharp ears. Two days later she asked, "Who is this Stanley you're always talking about? Is he in this school?"

"Stanley who?" said Jason, playing dumb.

"The one who eats so much ice cream. Somebody should tell him too much is not good for him. Or his cat Fluffy either."

The boys promised to tell Stanley and then chuckled all the way down the hall.

On Friday night, as Michael and Norman were wheeling the plants into the living room, Norman warned, "You have to stay out of the room so we can talk. And don't listen at the door!"

"I'm not interested in anything you and Bob talk about."

"And don't run in with any funny heads to scare us."

"You're the one who does that, not me."

"OK, but don't forget to put Fluffy's food out, and not too early, so Bob won't see it."

"Stop telling me what to do!" said Michael. "I'll feed Fluffy and Stanley at the same time."

"Well, don't put their sock pieces too close together. They might get into a fight. It's fudge ripple tonight, you know."

"Yeah, I'll watch out for dueling vines. If they start fighting, I'll get your Blaster and syrup them into submission."

When the doorbell rang, Norman ran to let Bob in. "What are we having to eat?" asked Bob.

"Pizza and popcorn," said Norman.

Bob's smile faded when he came into the living room. "What are your plants doing out here?"

Michael replied, "They're going to keep me company while I sleep on the couch."

"But I wanted to sleep in your room with the giant plants growing all over. Like sleeping in the jungle."

"Sorry," said Michael.

"Can we take one plant back in there? Like half a jungle?"

"No."

"Norman and I could sleep out here tonight."

"Nope," said Michael, "not tonight."

"Why not?"

"I have my reasons."

"Come on," said Norman. "We can tell scary ghost monster jungle stories." He and Bob ran down the hall.

At bedtime Bob overheard Mom out in the hall telling

Dad, "It's my turn to use the earplugs and your turn to get up if anything goes wrong."

"Goes wrong?" asked Bob, sticking his head out into the hall. "Is something going to go wrong?"

"No, of course not," she reassured him.

"If something might go wrong, I won't be able to go to sleep. Are you sure nothing will happen?"

"Relax, Bob. Everything will be fine. But if you wake up during the night, remember, please don't go anywhere except to the bathroom. No wandering around. OK? And if you need anything, be sure to wake up Norman."

"OK," said Bob. "I'll try not to worry."

Chapter 11

Two hours later bursts of laughter and the squeaking of beds being jumped on could be heard faintly down the hall in the living room.

Michael was lying on the couch watching a monster movie. He had shoved the couch across the hall doorway, put one plant at each end of the couch, and cut up some fudge ripple socks in plant-meal-size pieces.

Now, before he put the socks out, he was just waiting for silence from the boys to signal that they were finally falling alsleep. There was plenty of time before the plants usually ate, and he didn't want to take any chances of Bob accidentally coming out and wanting an explanation.

The glow from the TV set gave off plenty of eerie light. He had turned out the lamps so he wouldn't have to get up to do that when he was ready to go to sleep. Then he could just press the off button on the TV's remote control, which he put on the couch cushion next to him.

The sound was turned down very low, so Dad wouldn't come and tell him to turn it off. He could barely hear it.

He had seen the first part of this movie twice before, but because it was always on so late, he had fallen asleep in the middle of it both times. He had never seen the end.

Jason had seen it, though, and told him the part where the giant octopus tried to destroy Tokyo was great—with planes and tanks and electrical explosions, and the giant octopus's arms sneaking up and grabbing people.

Michael thought the octopus was a pretty good fake, slimy and purple-gray with mean yellow eyes. Its arms, full of huge suckers like the bottom of a bathtub non-skid shower mat, made wonderful gooshy noises as they sneaked up.

The movie kept stopping for more and more commercials. Michael, getting very sleepy, was determined to stay awake for the end this time, even if he had to prop his eyelids open with his fingers.

He nodded off during one commercial break, but woke up abruptly when the octopus appeared again. After the next break, however, he went on dozing. He did not hear Bob go out in the hall on his way to the bathroom.

What woke him was a feeling of something definitely odd going on. Then he realized something was crawling over his bare feet. He sat up with a start, yelling, "Octopus! Octopus!"

Then he started to giggle because his feet were being tickled. He was relieved to see it was only Stanley, feeling around with a vine to find the socks Michael had not yet put on the floor.

But Bob was already hurtling down the hall to see

what was wrong. He rounded the corner too fast to stop when the couch loomed in the doorway and flipped right over the back of it. As he bounced on the cushions, he hit the volume button on the remote control a couple of times.

Sound boomed out—planes dive-bombing, machine guns, explosions, people yelling, gooshy sneaking-up noises from the octopus arms, and blood-curdling screams from the evil scientist being dragged into the ocean by the monster.

Michael was now giggling uncontrollably as he tried to untangle Stanley's tickling vine from his feet.

Bob was somewhat stunned by the whole scene. From the eerie light of the TV screen a big mean yellow eye surrounded by purple-gray slime glared right at him. Bob screamed even better than the evil scientist in the movie.

Dad came running to the rescue. Because he was still half asleep, he forgot the couch was going to be moved and fell right over it. Norman came running, too.

When Dad saw the boys were all right, he blinked a few times. Then he realized the gunfire, dive-bombing, and explosions were not actually occurring in the living room.

"Turn that thing down!" he yelled, but the guns on the aircraft carrier the octopus was attacking were so loud nobody could hear him.

Now Norman was working on separating the vine curling affectionately around Michael's feet. Michael, still madly giggling, was feeling around between the couch cushions trying to find the remote control.

Suddenly an orchestra began blasting "The Star-Spangled Banner." The movie was over, and the station was going off the air for the night. Norman stood at attention, saluted the flag on the screen, and started singing along.

Dad stomped over to the TV and pulled the plug. The silence was amazing.

"Rats!" said Michael. "I missed the ending again. Did anybody see how it came out?"

"The octopus sank in the ocean," said Bob. "Maybe it isn't really dead and there'll be a sequel."

Dad looked around for socks and didn't see any. "You didn't notice anything unusual here, did you, Bob?" he asked casually.

"Just the octopus movie," Bob replied. "It was great! My mom and dad won't let me stay up to watch stuff like this. Wait till I tell them!"

"Wonderful," said Dad. He herded Bob and Norman back to bed. Michael put the socks out for the plants and went to sleep, thankful that Mom had slept through the whole thing with earplugs.

But she heard all about it in the morning—from Dad, from the neighbors who wondered why they were blasted awake at 2 A.M. by dive-bombing and "The Star Spangled Banner," and from Bob, who was thrilled by all the excitement. He could hardly wait to tell his parents when he got home.

Michael tried to reassure Mom with, "It was only a little uproar."

"In this family," she replied, "there is no such thing as only a little uproar."

To butter her up, Michael volunteered to make breakfast. He tried his imaginary fudge ripple pancake recipe, and it actually worked. Bob and Norman loved them. They took turns syrup blasting everyone's plate.

"That octopus movie was the best," said Bob. "I'm

going to write my letter to the editor about how kids should be allowed to stay up and watch monster movies.''

''You're writing to the newspaper?'' asked Mom.

''Our whole class is. The teacher told us yesterday to think of something we're for or against. Then Monday we're going to write our letters and send them to the paper.''

''Oh, yeah,'' said Dad, leafing through the newspaper. ''On Saturdays they usually run letters from kids. Here's one about being kind to animals and one about snowflakes.''

''Norman, you didn't mention that,'' said Mom.

''I told Fluffy. Besides, I didn't think of anything to write about yet.''

Bob suggested, ''You can write about syrup blasting.''

''Please, not that,'' said Mom. ''Promise me, Norman, that you won't write about anything weird.''

''Then I won't have anything to write about,'' he replied, pouting.

''I'm sure you'll be able to think of something non-weird by Monday,'' said Mom. ''Promise?''

''OK,'' he agreed grumpily.

When Bob left, he asked Norman if he could come back that night to sleep over again, but Mom said no, they would have to make it another time.

Closing the door behind him, she added, ''In about twenty years.''

''Now that Bob is gone,'' said Dad, ''we have something serious to discuss. I have some good news and some bad news.''

Michael started having that sinking feeling again.

''The good news,'' Dad continued, ''is that after two years of being too busy at work to take a vacation, I'm going to be able to take off three weeks next month.''

''Yay!'' shouted Norman. ''Where are we going?''

"Nowhere, unless we do something about the plants. That's the bad news. We can't leave them home alone for three weeks. And we can't have someone else come in to feed them socks."

"Let's take them along," said Norman. "Fluffy liked going for a walk. He'd love to take a vacation."

Mom explained, "The plants are too big to take anywhere. They won't fit in the car. Even if they did, there wouldn't be any room left for us."

"Jason could come over and feed them," said Michael. "He already knows about the socks and won't tell."

Mom argued, "One of his parents would have to drive him over every day. I don't think they'd let a kid go in an empty house by himself. I know I wouldn't. And what if he got sick and his parents had to take over? Then he'd have to tell them about the socks. It's just too risky."

"We could rent a pickup truck and take the plants over to Jason's house," said Norman.

"No, then his family would definitely find out."

"Besides," said Dad, "I don't completely trust that kid, not since he tried to blackmail Norman. If the plants produced seeds while he was alone with them, I don't think he could withstand the temptation to keep a few."

"So we have to face facts," said Mom. "Even though Fluffy and Stanley solved the messiness problem—and I'm grateful for that—they cause major uproars when someone spends the night here, and now they're keeping us from going on vacation. So your father and I have come up with a plan."

Even before he heard it, Michael knew he was not going to like it.

"We'll make smaller versions of them," Mom explained. "I'll take cuttings and root them. We won't feed them much so they won't get big so fast. Then we can take the little plants on vacation. They'll be so easy to carry."

"But what about Fluffy and Stanley?" asked Norman, looking worried.

"We'll have to get rid of the big ones, but you'll have Fluffy Junior and Stanley Junior. They'll be the same plants, only smaller and cuter."

"No!" shouted Norman. "I want the real Fluffy!"

Michael was furious. "This isn't fair," he protested. "We made a deal, and I've stuck to it. It's very hard for me to be neat all the time, but I'm doing it. And I've kept my promise not to tell about the socks. Even Norman has kept his mouth shut. Jason finding out was sort of Norman's fault, but . . ."

"Wait a minute!" squawked Norman.

"But," Michael continued, "he didn't mean to, so it wasn't exactly his fault."

"Right," said Norman, "I had to go to the bathroom."

Then Dad threw in the clincher. "You both have always wanted to go to Disney World. Wouldn't that make up for getting rid of the big plants when you have little ones to take along?"

Michael really wanted to go to Disney World. He thought about the great rides and getting his picture taken with Mickey Mouse. It was a hard decision.

"I want to stay home and keep Stanley," he said.

"Norman," said Mom, "what about you? You've always wanted to go there, and you'd have a cute little Fluffy Junior to take along."

Norman thought that over. "Can I take him on the rides?" he asked.

"No," said Dad, "he might fall off or get squashed

when you're going fast, but I'll hold him for you while you go on the rides.''

Norman's eyes lit up at that thought. He could see himself and Fluffy Junior getting their picture taken with Mickey or even Goofy. Fluffy was too big to fit in a picture like that and too big to go anywhere.

''What about the real Fluffy?'' he asked wistfully.

''When you have Fluffy Junior, you won't need the big one any more,'' said Mom.

''No way!'' yelled Norman, stomping out of the kitchen. Michael followed, wondering what to do about this new mess. He heard Dad ask, ''Does this mean I have to go to Disney World by myself?''

''Not without me,'' said Mom. ''I've always wanted to get my picture taken with Mickey. But first, what are we going to do about those blasted plants? Who's running this family anyway? Us or the kids?''

''Right now,'' said Dad, ''the plants.''

Chapter 12

"They're not going to give up," Michael told Norman. "It's time for a new master plan."

"What?"

"We'll just have to try everything we can think of and maybe one of them will work. There is one thing I can do that would save the plants for at least two and a half weeks. By then we could think of something else."

"Whatever it is," said Norman, "let's do it!"

"First thing Monday morning," said Michael, "I'll sign up Stanley and Fluffy as a project for the science fair."

"But Mom and Dad will never go for that."

"I won't tell them until after I sign up. They always encourage me to do well in school, so I'll just tell them my life will be ruined if I'm not in the science fair."

"I want to do something, too," said Norman.

"What about that letter you have to write?"

"You want me to write about our mean mom and dad forcing us to go to Disney World?"

"No, write about pet plants. If it gets in the paper about how wonderful Mom and Dad are to let you have a gigantic pet plant, then it would be too embarrassing for them to get rid of Fluffy—or Stanley, either."

"You think it might get in?"

"Sure, pet plants are a great idea. Even Jason thought so."

"OK, I'll try," said Norman. "But what if it doesn't get in the paper?"

"Don't worry. Before the science fair is over, we'll think of something else in case the letter doesn't get in, something really big."

Norman heaved a sigh of relief and patted Fluffy's leaves. "Don't worry," he told the plant. "Everything's going to be fine."

Michael hoped he was right.

As Norman left for school Monday, Mom asked, "What are you going to write your letter about?"

"It's a surprise," he said.

"I don't want any more surprises," said Mom.

"You'll like this one," he called as he ran out the door. "It's not weird!"

"But how are two big plants just standing there going to be a science project?" asked Jason when Michael told him the news.

"They're going to show how plants grow differently when you feed them differently."

"You're going to tell about the clean socks and dirty socks?"

"Of course not! Stanley is bigger because I kept putting bits of different food in his dirt. Fluffy didn't get

74

that. They both got socks. That isn't a difference, so I don't think I have to mention that part."

Jason looked unconvinced that this was a good idea. "This is probably not going to win anything," he said, "especially with what everybody else is doing."

"Yeah, I know Kimberly is building a computer, and Chad is making a relief map of the entire world, and you're doing the volcano. Isn't anybody doing anything simple?"

"Pat Jenkins is growing grass on a sponge the last I heard."

Michael said, "I know this isn't a very good project, but I want to save the plants, so I don't care. I didn't have any ideas for a project anyway. At least this way I've got something in the fair. That's better than nothing."

"But the science projects have to be here at school for three days. What are you going to do about feeding them socks in the middle of the night?"

"I'll think of something."

Mom and Dad did not take the news well when Michael told them at the dinner table.

"Why didn't you tell us before you did a crazy thing like this?" demanded Dad.

"Because I thought you might be a little upset," said Michael.

"UPSET!!!" yelled Mom. "Of course we're upset! How could you even think about taking those plants out in public?"

"Calm down," said Dad. "I'm sure Michael can substitute some other kind of science project."

"No, today was the last day to sign up, so I can't change my project now."

"There must be some rules to cover projects that fizzle out between sign-up day and the science fair."

Michael replied, "I can't think of anything else good. Jason is making a volcano that really works, and Kimberly Offenberg is building a computer, and Chad Palmer is doing a relief map of the entire world."

"Isn't anybody doing anything easy?" asked Mom.

"Pat Jenkins is growing grass on a sponge."

Norman piped up, "How is she going to mow it?

Mom said, "Norman, this is serious."

"Why doesn't she grow bean sprouts?" Norman continued, smirking. "You don't have to mow those."

Michael shoved him under the table so hard that Norman slid off his chair and disappeared from view.

While Norman thumped and bumped around under the table trying to get back up on his chair, Michael continued, "It's too late to change my project now, and my life will be ruined if I don't have something in the fair. You want me to do well in school, don't you?"

"Well, of course we do," said Dad. "But using those plants as a science project is ridiculous."

"No, it's not. There aren't going to be any problems. I promise."

"But," said Mom, "in the middle of the night they eat socks and Norman's makes funny noises."

Michael assured her, "There won't be anybody in the school at night. Nobody will find out."

"Are you sure?" asked Dad.

"Positive," said Michael.

"Then maybe it wouldn't do any harm," Dad told Mom.

"Well," said Mom doubtfully. "If you're sure nothing can go wrong. In the meantime I'll get the cuttings started for the junior plants so they'll be ready in time for our vacation."

After dinner she got a pair of scissors and headed for the boys' room.

"Fluffy isn't going to like this," warned Norman.

"This isn't going to hurt the plants, is it?" asked Michael.

"No, I'll just snip off a piece of each one. Then I'll put them in some special stuff I bought that makes cuttings grow roots. After that happens, we'll put them in pots and they'll grow. Don't worry. They'll be just like the big plants, only smaller."

She selected a sturdy little branch of Fluffy and snipped.

"Ow," said Norman, sounding like Fluffy.

Mom jumped. "Who said that?"

"Me," said Norman in the same funny voice.

"Norman, stop that!" ordered Mom.

"Who, me?" replied Norman innocently in his own voice.

Mom snipped a big piece off Stanley.

"GRRRRRR!" growled Michael in what he thought was a Stanley-like tone.

"You two better give up ventillakism. I mean, vantallaquism."

"Huh?" said Norman.

"You know what I mean," said Mom. "Knock it off."

As Michael was falling asleep, he sat up with a start. A horrible thought had just occurred to him. He had forgotten one big problem. The plants were too big to fit in the car. How was he going to get them to school?

He plopped back down on the pillow. If worse came to worst, they would have to roll them to the science fair on the skateboards. But this time of year was too cold for the plants to be outside very long.

He would have to find a better way. He fell asleep wondering how much it would cost to rent a truck.

Jason came to the rescue on the transportation problem. "My uncle Jim runs a limousine service," he explained. "I could talk him into taking the plants to school in one of those stretch limos, the really long kind. The seats fold over, so Fluffy and Stanley could ride lying down. That big limo is so long, I'm sure they'd fit."

"That would be perfect," said Michael. "But are you sure your uncle would do it? And how much would it cost?"

"He'd do it for free if I asked him," Jason assured him. "Just dropping the plants off at school wouldn't take long."

"Great!" exclaimed Michael. "I'll trade you something really good for this."

"That's OK, you don't have to do that," said Jason.

Michael thought that Jason passing up a trade was very odd.

Then Jason added casually, "But maybe some day if the plants ever grow seeds, you could give me a couple of those."

"My mom and dad would have a fit if I did that," said Michael. "Besides, Mom says if they haven't grown seeds by now, they probably never will."

"So if that's probably not going to happen," said Jason, "making a deal for seeds wouldn't matter, would it?"

"I guess not."

"Wait till you see the limo!" said Jason. "Your neighbors will think Fluffy and Stanley are going to a prom!"

During the days before the science fair, Mom kept tending the cuttings, but Michael kept pouring strange things on them, like soft drinks and salt water, when Mom was not looking. The cuttings were not doing very well.

Dad and Mom were both surprised about the limo that Jason had arranged, but they did not object. "Since we're stuck with this science project, we might as well make the best of it," Mom decided. "We do want Michael to do well in school, and the boys are going to have to give up the plants soon. So if this will make them happy, why not?"

"You're right," said Dad. "The night we take the plants to school, let's go early and then take the kids out for pizza to cheer them up."

On the big night the longest shiniest black car Michael had ever seen pulled up in front of the house. The boys carefully rolled the plants to the curb.

Jason's uncle Jim, wearing a black suit and visored cap, helped the family ease the plants into the limo without crunching them. Norman wriggled far into the back seat to guide them from that end.

Dad and Mom got into the family car and pulled out of the drive to lead the way to school. Uncle Jim and Michael crammed themselves into what little space was left in the limo's front seat, and they drove off with leaves and vines sticking out every window.

In the back seat Norman, wearing the gorilla head, waved merrily to passing people in cars.

People stared. Children waved. Cars screeched to a halt as the little jungle on wheels went by.

Quite a crowd gathered when the limo pulled up in front of the school and the driver, one boy, and one small gorilla got out, carefully wrestled two huge plants out, and rolled them up the school's front walk.

Dad caught up with Norman and made him take the gorilla head off before they went in.

In the gym they found the table with Michael's number at the end of a long row. They managed to get the skateboards off, and hoisted the plants up on the table.

Michael set up his signs and report explaining the project.

Mom arranged the plants to show their best sides and polished some of the leaves.

Dad got some water for them from a drinking fountain.

Norman went behind the table, put on his gorilla head, and popped up between the plants. He surprised the custodian and three teachers.

The exhibit to the left of Michael's was a big model of a dam full of real water. The table on the right was still empty.

When they were ready to leave, Mom, Dad, and Norman stood in front of the plants and made sure no one was looking while Mom took two socks out of her purse and slipped them to Michael. He put a dirty white one behind Stanley where he hoped it would not be noticed. Next to Fluffy he put a clean brown and white striped one. Norman had insisted on fudge ripple.

The whole family did not stay long to look at other projects on their way out. "We'll see them all when we come back Friday night," said Dad. "Right now it's time for pizza."

At the restaurant Norman went under the table to put on his gorilla head to surprise the waitress.

"We'll have a large pepperoni with everything," Dad ordered.

"And what will your gorilla have?" asked the waitress.

Chapter 13

With the plants gone, the boy's room seemed very empty. "I miss Fluffy," said Norman.

"I know what you mean," said Michael. "We've only got two more days. Tomorrow is the judging. The next day the science fair is open to the public. Then it'll be all over. And so will our plants unless we do something fast."

He dropped his socks on the floor, knowing they would still be there in the morning.

"You're getting messy again," yelped Norman. "I wish Stanley was here to keep after you!"

"That's it! For once you've got a good idea."

"What?"

"We'll both be messy to show Mom and Dad what this room will be like without our plants. I know this will be hard for a neatness nut like you, but I'll give you messy lessons. You're lucky to have an expert like me for a brother."

Before Norman could complain about this, Mom came in to say good night.

"Michael, pick up your socks," she added.

"If Stanley and Fluffy were here," he replied, "I wouldn't be able to forget to pick up my socks."

"The junior plants will do the job," said Mom firmly. "Now get to bed. It's getting late."

After she went out, Norman whispered, "Now what are we going to do?"

"I don't know yet," said Michael.

After the lights were out, Michael thought he heard a little sniffling in the dark.

"Don't worry," he said. "We'll think of something." The sniffling stopped.

Next morning in the school hall Pat Jenkins walked up to Michael. Out of her bookbag she pulled a brown and white striped sock. "Is this yours?" she asked.

"Where did you find that?"

"The end was sticking out of your exhibit last night."

"What made you think it was mine?"

"Your name is on that strange plant project. If this sock isn't yours, then somebody must have left it there. When I saw it, I knew you wouldn't want something like that lying around making your project look messy. So I picked it up for you."

"Uh, thanks."

"I knew you'd be glad," said Pat. "See you later."

So Fluffy had had nothing to eat last night. Michael hoped the plant was all right, but the gym would not be open until noon for anyone who needed to tend to science projects. He would have to wait until then to find out.

As he leaned over the water fountain to get a drink,

he heard the custodian talking to the principal, Mr. Leedy.

"I know this sounds impossible, but after everybody left last night and the lights were out in the gym, I went back there to empty the trash can by the door. And I heard something that sounded just like a burp."

"A burp?" asked Mr. Leedy.

"Definitely a burp," said the custodian. "Then I heard another burp. And then," he lowered his voice to a whisper, "somebody or something said 'ex.' "

Michael's finger slipped and squirted the drinking fountain all over his nose.

"Ex?" said Mr. Leedy.

"Definitely ex," said the custodian.

"Who was it?"

"Nobody. I turned on all the lights and looked all over."

"Maybe the heating system was making funny noises again."

"No, the heating system has never burped."

"Let's just keep this to ourselves," said Mr. Leedy, "so we don't alarm anyone until we find out what caused it. We don't want any kids jumping to the silly conclusion that the gym is haunted or anything like that. It's probably only a chemical reaction in one of the science projects."

"I don't think so," said the custodian.

Michael sped off down the hall as fast as he could without running. There were a few minutes left until the bell rang, so he hurried over to the side of the building where Norman's classroom was. He waved at him to come out in the hall.

"There were two burps and one ex," Michael explained. "I know what Stanley had to eat, but what did Fluffy eat?"

"Uh-oh," said Norman.

"Uh-oh is right," said Michael. "I'm afraid to look."

After lunch he went to the gym with the others who needed to check on their science projects.

At the door he ran into Pat Jenkins. "How did your grass on a sponge turn out?" he asked, hoping she would not bring up the subject of socks again.

"I decided that was too easy, so I collected herbs and nature things that make different dyes and showed what colors they make."

"You dyed a bunch of material?"

"No, white socks."

Michael turned at the row where his project was. He hoped Pat would not turn there, too. She did.

"I used socks," she explained, "because later we're going to wear them with costumes in my creative dramatics class. The kids playing frogs will wear the green ones and the ones playing goldfish . . ."

She stopped at the space next to Michael's which had been empty last night.

"Somebody swiped one of my socks!" she exclaimed.

"Hmmm," said Michael, trying to think of what to say.

"How dumb!" she went on. "Why would anybody swipe a sock out of a person's science project? This is going to look terrible to the judges with that empty space right at the top!"

"What color was it?" he asked. The rest were the yukkiest colors he had ever seen.

"White, to show what they all looked like before I dyed them."

Michael offered, "I'll get you that sock you gave me this morning to fill up your empty spot."

"No, that had brown stripes. I need a plain white sock."

Michael sighed and took off his shoe. "Take one of my mine until you can get another one."

"That's really nice of you. But why are you doing this?"

"I know how I'd feel if something happened to my project," he replied.

"OK, thanks. I'll give it back tomorrow. Wait till I get my hands on whoever did this. This is very mysterious. I'll bet it has something to do with that sock I found on your table last night."

Michael said, "You aren't going to tell anyone about this, are you? It all sounds so weird."

Pat stuck the white sock up on the pieces of tape where the missing one had been. "There! It looks as good as new!"

At the door Michael took off his other sock and put it in his back pocket. Now if anyone noticed his ankles, at least they would match.

When the judges talked to the students at each exhibit, they were very impressed with the model dam and Pat's display.

To Michael the head judge said, "Those plants certainly are—uh—very unusual looking." Michael answered his questions about feeding methods. But he did not mention the socks part of the menu.

"Very—ah—interesting," said the judge, writing on his clipboard. Then he looked at Michael oddly.

"One of that bigger plant's vines seems to be stuck in your back pocket," he said.

Startled, Michael jumped sideways, bumping into the edge of the table that held the dam. Its water began sloshing back and forth.

He reached out to steady it. But the vine was still in his pocket with a firm grip on the sock there. As he jumped and leaned over, that jerked the huge plant hard enough to pull it off balance. It began to topple over.

The judge reached out with both hands to keep it from crashing, tossing aside his clipboard. It plopped into the dam. Water splashed in every direction.

Michael, the plants, and the judge stood there dripping little puddles.

"You should have brought your umbrella," said the custodian, as he went off, chuckling, to get paper towels and a mop.

Michael helped the judge spread his soaked papers on the floor to dry. Then he went to get water to refill the dam.

The custodian gave him a pail to use. After he filled it, the custodian said, "Let me carry that, kid, just to be on the safe side. I don't want any more floods in here."

Michael gladly handed it over.

As the custodian approached the dam and lifted the heavy pail to pour, he skidded on a wet paper. Trying to keep his balance, he let go of the pail. It thunked down on the floor and slopped water all over him.

"You should have worn your galoshes," said the judge.

"I think this exhibit table has a curse on it," said the custodian.

As he turned to go get more paper towels, he stepped on a double skateboard that had jarred loose from under the table when the pail thunked so hard on the floor. The astonished custodian rolled away down the aisle. His screams grew fainter as he disappeared through the gym doors out into the hall.

"Uh-oh," said Michael. He and the judge ran out to see what had happened. They found the custodian safely holding on to the drinking fountain, which he had grabbed to stop himself.

"Kid, your project is a hazard to the whole science fair," he said.

"They're just a couple of plants," said Michael, going to retrieve the skateboard, which had rolled to the end of the hall.

"They're not normal," said the custodian. "Mark my words. Something else is going to go wrong."

After the judges were finished with Pat's project, Michael told her he was leaving two socks next to his plants for a special reason and not to touch them.

"I get it," she said. "They'll be bait in case the sock swiper strikes again tonight. You want whoever it is to take those instead of mine. What a good idea! That's really nice of you."

"That's OK," said Michael. "Just don't say anything about it to anybody."

Pat asked, "Do you think the sock swiper left that brown and white striped sock by mistake?"

"I don't think so."

He went to find Jason. He was staring glumly at his volcano, which was surrounded by runny globs of gray goo.

"How did things go with the judging?" asked Michael.

"My lava flowed so well it unfortunately flowed all over the judge's shoes."

"Mine didn't go too well either," said Michael. "But that's still a great looking volcano."

"Your plants are great, too," said Jason. "Everybody's talking about them. Too bad your mom and dad want to get rid of them."

"Yeah, but I haven't given up trying. I think that maybe if we made a giant mess in our room it'd show them how it'd be without big plants."

"Would that work?"

"Only if it was a big enough mess to convince them. What we need is something spectacular—a major all-out mess—so much junk they won't be able to see the furniture. A junkathon!"

Jason grinned. "I'll help! We can go around the neighborhoods on trash night and haul home any big stuff left out for pickup on the tree lawns."

"Then we'd just have to find some place to hide all of it until the junkathon."

"How about a neighbor's garage?" suggested Jason.

After school Michael explained the junkathon to Norman. He wrinkled his nose. "Do we have to? I hate messiness! Ugh! But I'll do it for Fluffy. And Stanley, too."

"We're desperate," said Michael. "Your letter hasn't been in the paper, so this is our last chance!"

"OK, what do we do?"

"First, we have to find a neighbor who will let us use their garage to hide the junk while we collect it."

"What about Mrs. Smith?" Norman suggested. "She's already got half a garage full of stuff. She's getting ready for a garage sale."

"Aha!" exclaimed Michael. "Better still, maybe we could borrow her junk. You ask her. She likes you."

Mrs. Smith was willing, but she wanted to know why Norman wanted to borrow her things.

"It's a surprise for my mom and dad," explained Norman.

"But I've already starting putting price stickers on for the sale. Will that matter?"

"No, that's fine," Norman replied. He ran off to tell Michael the good news before Mrs. Smith could ask him to explain further.

Chapter 14

On the last day of the science fair, Mom said, "We still have to figure out how to get rid of the plants."

"I arranged for Jason's uncle to come by with the limo at the end of the fair tonight to pick them up," said Dad. "He didn't want to take any money, because he said the plants attracted so much attention he's gotten a lot of new business. But I insisted on paying him. He's been such a big help in this whole mess."

"Where is he taking them? To the city trash dump?"

"No, that's twenty miles away and only city trash trucks can get in there, not limos. We'll have to bring them home and then put them out on the curb on regular trash pickup day. The boys will be happy to keep them a few more days."

"But," Mom argued, "some innocent person who likes big plants might take them before the trash truck gets here. Or the trash men might save them. We can't take a chance on that."

Dad suggested, "How about tying notes to them that say, 'Caution, this plant could be hazardous to your socks'?"

"Be serious. Maybe we'll have to pour weed killer on them or chop them up in little pieces."

"I don't want to be the one to do it," said Dad.

"Neither do I," said Mom.

Michael, who had been listening in the next room, casually strolled in. He asked, "How are the junior plants coming along?"

"Terrible," said Mom. "I don't know what's wrong."

"We can't throw out the big ones until the junior ones are growing well," said Michael. "What if the little ones die or don't grow? You'd need the big ones for more cuttings."

"Well, I suppose a few more days won't hurt," said Mom.

That evening at the public showing of the science fair, Michael and Norman lined up in front of Stanley and Fluffy while Dad took pictures.

Norman looked at the trophy the dam had won and the blue ribbon on the socks display. "How come our plants didn't win anything?" he asked.

"You must be kidding," said Michael. "I was just glad to have something in the fair and save the plants a little longer."

"How many points did the judges give us?"

"Not many. Most of them got washed away when the judge's clipboard fell in the dam. He was using a felt pen, and the numbers ran all over the paper."

"Too bad," said Norman, "they don't give a prize for the weirdest. We would have won that."

"I think this is one of the best exhibits," said Dad. "I'm proud of both of you."

"Me, too," said Mom. "It's really too bad these plants are just too much trouble to keep."

The principal, Mr. Leedy, came by. "Your son's project certainly is—ah—unusual. I've never seen plants like these before. They've attracted a lot of attention, perhaps because they're the tallest exhibit. Or perhaps because they arrived in a limo."

"Be careful," said the custodian, coming up behind him. "This is the area I was telling you about. And watch out for skateboards that sneak up on you."

"Looks all right to me," answered Mr. Leedy as they walked away together.

"It's not," said the custodian. "Last night I heard a couple of schlurps and then later two more burps and another 'ex' from this corner. I think it definitely might be haunted."

"Keep your voice down," warned Mr. Leedy.

Michael's teacher came by. "I've had my eye on these plants all during the science fair," she said. "I want you to tell me later, Michael, everything you did to make them grow this big. I'd love to get mine to grow like this."

Pat Jenkins hurried up the aisle looking excited. "Those socks you left last night were gone today! You saved my project from the phantom sock swiper!"

"You didn't tell anybody, did you?" asked Michael.

"I told everybody! My teacher hasn't had a chance to do anything about it yet, so just now when I was out in the hall I saw Mr. Leedy talking to the custodian. So I reported it to him, too. If anyone can find the joker who's doing this, the principal can."

"What did he say?"

"Nothing. But he got the funniest look on his face. And then the custodian said 'I told you so.' He told Mr.

91

Leedy he should call in a ghost hunter right away. Wait till I tell everybody. Of course, I don't believe in ghosts. Do you suppose this gym could be haunted?''

"I don't think so,'' said Michael. "Congratulations on winning a ribbon.''

"If you hadn't helped me out with a sock, I probably wouldn't have won anything. So when I take my exhibit down, I'm going to give you a pair of my specially dyed socks. Which two colors would you like?''

"No, you already thanked me. That's enough.'' He escaped into the crowd.

In the limo on the way home, Norman put on his gorilla head again to wave to everyone they passed. He hoped this would not be Fluffy's and Stanley's last ride. But he was looking forward to Michael's big junkathon plan to save the day. And tomorrow was Saturday, one more chance that his letter might be in the paper.

Norman got up so early Saturday morning that he was waiting on the front step in his pajamas and robe when the paper boy arrived.

"I have to see if my letter is in,'' he explained. The paper boy looked through the newspaper with him.

It was there! They read it together:

"Some kids can't have dogs and cats and snakes for pets. Their moms won't let them. You can't have pets in an apartment. Pets make some people sneeze. They should get plants to be pets. Plants don't make you sneeze. Plants don't get hairs on the chairs. A plant does not bark loud or get lost. Plants are good pets.''

Norman felt thrilled to see his words and name in print.

"This is a good idea,'' said the paper boy. "I think

I'll get one of those pet plants myself. See ya!'' He sped off on his bike.

Norman raced into the house and tickled Michael's feet to wake him. ''Stanley, stop that,'' mumbled Michael.

''Wake up! My letter's in the paper!'' exclaimed Norman.

Michael sat up and read it. ''But where's the part about wonderful Mom and Dad? The part that was going to embarrass them into letting us keep our plants?''

''I wrote it in my letter, but it's not there. My teacher said sometimes the editors leave parts out if they don't have enough room.''

''This is a good letter,'' said Michael, ''but it's not going to work on Mom and Dad. So I guess we're stuck with going ahead on the junkathon. I'm going back to sleep.''

Norman tore across the hall to wake his parents. A groggy Dad read the letter to Mom.

''That's wonderful,'' said Mom. ''I'm so proud of you, Norman.''

''See my name right there?'' he said, bouncing up and down on their bed.

''Stop that,'' said Dad. ''You're making me seasick. This is a great letter. I'll bet one or two people will actually get pet plants as a result of what you wrote.''

Mom squinted at the clock. ''It's 6 A.M.,'' she announced.

''Yeah,'' said Norman, ''I knew you'd want to get up right away to see my letter.''

''Yes, and now that I've seen it, I'm going back to sleep. We'll celebrate later.''

''Aren't you going to get up and call Grandma and everybody else to tell them about my letter?''

"Wake me up in two hours, and we'll do it then," said Mom with her eyes closed.

"Me, too," said Dad, snuggling back down under the covers.

Norman was too excited to go back to bed. It was too early to call up Bob, so he talked to Fluffy for a while and read his letter out loud three times. He picked out just the right place on the wall to hang up his letter after he got it framed. On second thought, maybe the refrigerator door would be better. More people would see it there.

Later there were several phone calls from people who had seen Norman's letter. Bob came over and was invited to stay for breakfast. Then Norman called Grandma long distance and told her all about it.

That afternoon Mom and Dad went out to do Saturday errands and get photocopies made of Norman's letter to send to all the relatives. Norman went over to Bob's, so when the phone rang, Michael answered.

"This is Kim Christopher from Channel Two News. Are you the boy who wrote the letter in this morning's paper about the pet plants?"

"That's my brother. He's not home right now, but he'll be back soon."

"Could I speak to your mother or father, please?"

"They're not here, but they'll be back any minute."

"I need to talk to them about interviewing your brother. To do it in time for the six o'clock news we'll have to come over there by three."

If Norman and the plants were on TV, Michael thought, they would be famous. Then Mom and Dad could never force them to get rid of pet plants that everyone had seen on TV. And then he could call off the junkathon. Maybe he would be on TV, too. That would be great.

"Three o'clock would be OK," he said.

"You're sure this is all right with your parents? We need their permission."

"Oh, yes, it'll be fine with them." If it wasn't, he wondered as he hung up, how could he ever talk himself out of the big trouble he was going to be in?

Chapter 15

"TV? Here?" asked Dad when he got home. "Where's Norman?"

"I called him at Bob's," said Michael. "He'll be right home. The TV people will be here in a few minutes."

The front door flew open. Norman zoomed in and started jumping up and down. "TV! TV! I'm going to be on TV!"

Mom grabbed him. "Wash your face! Put on a clean shirt! Comb your hair! Tie your shoelaces!"

Norman ran off with shoelaces flapping. Mom dashed around picking up newspapers and other things strewn around the living room. She shoved everything under the couch. Dad followed with the vacuum cleaner roaring.

Michael answered the door. Kim Christopher marched in and introduced the cameraman who was lugging all the equipment.

"How about two chairs in front of the fireplace for a

nice homey background?'' she asked him. ''The kid can sit right there with his little plant on his lap, and I'll sit here.''

''Fine,'' said the cameraman, ''but we'll have to move this couch out of the way.''

''We're not moving the couch,'' said Mom. ''The plants are in the boys' room. You can do the interview in there.''

''But kids' rooms look so messy,'' said Kim.

''Theirs is always neat,'' said Mom.

''That's unusual,'' replied Kim.

Norman reappeared in a dress-up shirt and good pants. His hair was neatly slicked down, and he smelled wonderful. Even from ten feet away, Michael's nose recognized Dad's best aftershave lotion. Norman must have used half the bottle. Michael was tempted to tell him this was only for television, not smellevision, but he kept quiet.

''You must be little Norman,'' said Kim. ''I loved your letter.''

Norman glared up at her. He did not like being called little.

The cameraman said, ''Show us your plant. We don't have much time, and if it's too small to show up well, we'll have to do some close-up shots.''

Norman led the way to the plants.

''Mine is called Fluffy,'' he said proudly.

At the sight of the towering greenery, Kim said, ''This is going to be a little different from what I had in mind.''

While the cameraman set up, she explained, ''Now, Norman, we'll just stand here in front of the plants and talk. I'll read your letter, and then ask you about having a pet plant. OK? Now don't be nervous. We'll just pretend the camera and microphone and lights are not here, and that you're just talking to me, not the hundreds of thousands of people who'll be watching."

"OK," said Norman, looking petrified.

"And then I'll get a few comments from your mom and dad and brother, and it'll be all over."

"Ready?" asked the cameraman. Kim nodded, and the blinding lights went on.

Kim turned to the camera. "These two huge plants don't look like your average family pets, but there's a boy who thinks differently. He says plants make wonderful pets."

Mom was behind the cameraman waving at Norman to stand up straight. He did.

"So he wrote this letter to the newspaper," Kim continued. She read it to the camera. Norman looked pleased at the sound of his own words.

"Norman, why did you decide to get a plant for a pet?"

"I already had the plant, and then I decided it should be my pet." He looked stiff with nervousness. Mom did sign language at him to smile. He did.

"Does your plant have a name?"

"Yes."

"Well, what is it?"

"You know."

"What do you call it?"

"I already told you. Fluffy." Norman was still smiling, but he looked strange.

"How adorable! Why did you choose that name?"

"Because he's sort of like a cat to me."

"You mean you always wanted a cat, but your mom and dad wouldn't let you have one, so your plant is the substitute for the cuddly little kitty they wouldn't let you have."

"No," said Norman, looking puzzled and still smiling stiffly.

"At least it doesn't shed hair all over or make a lot of noise meowing," said Kim, laughing merrily at her own witty remarks.

"No," said Norman, "it never gets hair on the furniture."

"Cut," said Kim. "Why do you have that strange look on your face?"

Norman reached a finger up to rearrange his mouth back to normal. "My top lip got stuck on my teeth when I smiled. Then I couldn't unsmile."

"Never mind," said Kim, glancing at her watch. "We don't have time to do it over. Now both you boys stand here between the plants. We need some action. You can be watering them."

Michael got a pitcher. Norman stepped into his half of the closet and came out with his Blaster.

"No," whispered Dad.

"I'll only pretend," Norman whispered back.

"How cute!" said Kim. "You water your plant with a giant water pistol! Hold that up so we get a good shot of it. Not like that. Like this!" She grabbed the end of the Blaster.

"Oops," said Norman.

"Ugh," said Kim. Her hand was dripping goo.

"I'm so sorry about that," said Mom. "Don't worry about your clothes. The syrup washes right out." She looked down. "I'm sure it'll come right off your shoes, too, real easily."

The cameraman asked, "Why does he have syrup in a water pistol?"

"It's too complicated to explain," said Dad.

While Mom helped Kim clean up, the cameraman

took some shots of the boys pretending to water the plants.

"Too bad they don't do anything besides just stand there," joked the cameraman. "It would be great if they'd come to life like in a monster movie and do something weird. Now that would be news!"

Michael and Norman laughed merrily.

Mom and Dad were next. Kim shoved a microphone at Dad. "How did this pet plant thing get started?"

"It just grew. Or rather the plants did, and then the boys got very attached to them. They didn't start out as pets."

"So now they're like beloved members of your family."

"Uh, well, the boys certainly are. Not the plants."

"You're against your son's plants for pets idea?"

"No, but . . ."

Kim turned the mike to Mom. "Are you in favor of plants for pets?"

"Yes, but . . ."

"What are the advantages of a family having plant pets instead of animals?"

"They're very neat," said Mom. "They don't eat much, or make a mess. They don't have to be walked."

"Eat?" asked Kim.

"Plant food," said Mom.

"Those plants are so big, I'll bet they eat plenty of plant food," said Kim. "It's a good thing they don't eat anything else!" She and Mom laughed merrily.

Kim grabbed Michael's arm and dragged him close to the mike. "How do you feel about your little brother's plant idea?" she asked.

"It's great. Not everybody can have an animal pet, but anybody can take care of a plant."

Kim pulled the mike away, but Michael clutched it

and babbled on. "We're very happy with our pets, and our mom and dad know they mean a lot to us. You can really care about a plant. It's like having a green friend. Everybody should have one. Any kid out there who's always wanted a pet but can't have one should get a plant. And so should everybody else."

"Cut," said Kim, winning the microphone tug-of-war. "That's enough. We're not doing a mini-series here."

"Let's go," said the cameraman. "It's going to take some extra time to edit all this down to make sense."

On her way out of the house, Kim Christopher muttered, "Thank goodness we weren't doing this live."

As they drove away, Norman exclaimed, "Being on TV is harder than I thought!"

Michael threw himself on the couch and shouted, "I'm going to look like an idiot on TV where everybody can see me."

"That's all right," said Dad. "We're all going to look like idiots together."

"Maybe nobody we know will be watching that channel tonight," said Mom.

Norman piped up, "Bob's mom said she was going to call all the neighbors about me being on TV."

"Uh-oh," said Michael.

Chapter 16

By the time they turned on the six o'clock news, they were all feeling calmer. They sat through the general news, weather, sports, and many commercials. As they impatiently watched a singing cereal box do a tap dance, Dad said, "There are only two minutes left."

"Aren't we going to be on?" asked Norman, very disappointed.

"Maybe they changed their minds. Maybe it was the syrup," said Michael, disappointed, too.

"After we went through all that, we're not going to be on?" said Mom indignantly. "How could they do that?"

Then the anchorman said, "And now, on a lighter note, here's Kim Christopher with a heartwarming story about a new kind of pet. Kim?"

"That's us," screamed Norman. Michael felt a lump in his throat. His hands were cold and damp.

Kim Christopher appeared to be standing in a jungle.

"These two huge plants don't look like your average family pets," she said, "but here's a boy who thinks differently. He says plants make wonderful pets."

As she read Norman's letter, he appeared, looking stupefied with fright. His head did not move, but his eyes went to the right. Suddenly he stood up very straight.

"Why did you decide to get a plant for a pet?"

"I already had the plant, and then I decided it should be my pet." His eyes went to the right again. Suddenly he smiled.

"What do you call it?"

"Fluffy."

"Didn't they leave something out there?" asked Dad.

"Shhh," said Mom. "Norman's going to talk again."

On the screen Kim said, "How adorable. Why did you choose that name?"

"Because he's sort of like a cat to me."

"At least it doesn't shed hair all over or make a lot of noise meowing." Kim laughed merrily.

"Didn't they leave out the cuddly kitty part?" asked Dad.

"Yes, thank goodness," said Mom.

Now the boys were pretending to water their plants as Kim's voice said, "Norman's brother Michael also loves his pet plant. Their mother and father love the plants, too."

"I didn't say that," said Dad.

"Shhh," said Mom.

"How did this pet plant thing get started?" asked Kim.

Dad mumbled into the microphone, "It just grew."

Dad groaned at the sight. "I knew I should have shaved and put on a tie!"

104

Mom appeared on the screen saying, "They're very neat. They don't eat much or make a mess."

Kim commented, "Those plants are so big, I'll bet they eat plenty of plant food. It's a good thing they don't eat anything else!"

Next Michael in a closeup said, "It's like having a green friend. Everybody should have one. Any kid out there who always wanted a pet but couldn't have one should get a plant."

Kim reappeared at the anchor desk. "So, Bill," she continued, "little Norman may have started a trend. Plants as pets may turn out to be a growing thing." She and Bill laughed merrily.

Michael felt relieved. They hadn't looked nearly as bad as he thought they would. Some of the dumbest parts were cut out. Now he wished he had called Jason and some of his other friends to tell them to watch.

"My hair looked awful," said Mom, "but we didn't sound too bad."

"We all looked fat," said Norman, "but Fluffy and Stanley looked good."

"Fat?" said Mom. "Fat!"

The phone started ringing. It seemed as if everyone they knew had seen them on TV. Neighbors dropped by to talk about it. Between answering the phone and the door, they had no chance to fix or eat dinner.

"I'm hungry," complained Norman after an hour and a half of this. "Can I make popcorn?"

"Let's go out for pizza," said Michael.

"Great idea," said Mom. "And on the way home, we can stop at Save-A-Lot. We're almost out of socks, and I forgot to buy any this afternoon."

"I don't want to go in there again," said Michael. "It's not my turn."

"We'll all go in together," said Dad.

*   *   *

At the pizza place several people came over to their table to say that they'd seen them on TV and liked the pet plant idea.

When they got to the Save-A-Lot, they had to drive around the parking lot three times to find a space.

"I didn't think Saturday was such a popular night to shop," said Dad.

Inside, every checkout counter had a line of customers buying plants. Voices of parents and children swarming around in the plant section could be heard all over the store.

"I want this one!"

"No, that's too big. We'll get a little one, and it will grow."

"I want that green one!" whined another little voice.

"Which one? They're all green!"

"Mommy, mommy, this one wants to come home with me!"

"This is the best idea," said one mother to another. "I know my kids would fizzle out on taking care of a dog and I'd get stuck with it. But I don't mind getting stuck with a plant."

A father asked a passing clerk, "Don't you have any big ones like that family on TV? We want something gigantic, not these dinky ones."

"Plants will grow larger, sir," said the clerk.

Michael, Mom, and Dad picked out the socks and were heading for the checkout counter when Michael noticed Norman was no longer following them. He found him among the crowd in the plant aisle. Standing up very straight and smiling, he seemed to be waiting to be recognized.

"Come on, we're leaving," said Michael. Dragging

his feet as slowly as possible, Norman followed him to the checkout line.

The four of them waiting in line together did get noticed. A little girl pointed and whispered to her father, who asked, "Hey, aren't you the pet plant people from TV?"

Norman stood up straight and smiled winningly. "That's us!" he said proudly.

People gathered around, talking about seeing them on TV and what a good idea pet plants were. Word spread throughout the store.

The checkout clerk was glad to see them. "The socks family!" she exclaimed. "It's nice to see you all together for a change. And now you're the pet plant people, too?"

"We were on TV," Norman told her. "And my letter was in the paper."

"Good for you," said the clerk. "You've done wonders for our plant sales. Our other branches are having a plant boom, too. There are going to be a lot of happy kids who never had pets before."

A few people followed them all the way out to the car to talk. They had not attracted so much attention since Norman wore the gorilla head to the science fair.

On the way home Michael asked, "Now that our plants are famous, we can keep them, right?"

"No," said Dad. "We're going on vacation, and you'll learn to love your little plants."

Monday morning the school halls were abuzz with talk of pet plants. By the time Michael got to his classroom he had heard all about Spot, an African violet, Greenie, a pot of ivy, Phil, a philodendron, and Woof-Woof, a geranium.

Pat Jenkins told him she had planted some marigold seeds but hadn't named them yet.

Jason said, "I got a snake plant, and I'm trying to decide whether to call it Scaly or Fangs."

"Definitely Fangs," said Michael. "Does it look like a snake?"

"Nope," said Jason, "but it might if snakes were flat and green with pointed heads and were standing up."

"Then why is it called a snake plant?"

"I don't know," said Jason, "but I always wanted a snake."

Michael explained to him that the junkathon was going to have to be after school Wednesday, because Mom did not get home from her part-time job until six that day.

Jason agreed to go home with Michael and Norman after school and arrange for his mother to pick him up there.

"Norman is going to get Bob to help, too," said Michael. "With four of us carrying things, it shouldn't take very long."

"Are your mom and dad ever going to be surprised," said Jason.

Wednesday, as school was letting out, Mr. Leedy stopped Michael in the hall. "I tried to call your home, but there was no answer," he said, "so would you take a message to your parents?"

"Sure," said Michael. He told Jason, "You go ahead with Norman and Bob. I'll catch up." He followed the principal into his office.

"We've been amazed at this pet plant movement you and your brother started," said Mr. Leedy.

"I'm amazed, too," said Michael.

"Who would have thought," continued Mr. Leedy,

"that those two—uh—unusual looking plants you had in the science fair would lead to such a good thing?"

"Yes," said Michael, wishing he would get to the point.

"So the teachers and I have been discussing this, and we've come up with a wonderful idea. We're going to have a Pet Plants Day after school starts next fall. We're starting to plan now so it will be really big."

Mr. Leedy paced back and forth with enthusiasm. "All the pupils who have pet plants can bring them to school that day. We'll have special science units planned in all the grades about plants and how to take care of them. Then we'll have a school open house that night so everyone can show off their plants. Doesn't that sound great?"

"Yes!" said Michael.

"So, of course," said Mr. Leedy, "we're going to give your whole family awards for starting this idea. We'll need you to bring your plants to be on display for the whole thing. So I need to find out if your parents can both come and bring the plants that day. They'll be much too big for a limo by then, so we'll send a large truck to pick them up."

"Great," said Michael.

"If that date is not OK with your folks, then we'll change the day, but we need to know right away. Would you have your mother or father call me tomorrow?"

Michael was delighted. How could Mom and Dad turn this down? Surely they would have to give up on the dumb junior plants idea and let them keep Stanley and Fluffy for this big event.

Now he could cancel the junkathon if this would save the plants. What a relief! He had not been looking forward to having to clean up all that junk when it was over.

He slid off his chair and started edging toward the door. "Let me tell you about the rest of the big plans for this," continued Mr. Leedy. He talked on and on.

Michael kept glancing at the wall clock. He hoped Jason, Norman, and Bob had not started to lug the junk into the house without him. But even if they had, there was still time to undo it before Mom and Dad got home.

He finally got up the nerve to interrupt Mr. Leedy. "Excuse me, can I use the phone to call home? I have to tell my brother something in a hurry, and he must be home by now."

"Of course," said Mr. Leedy. "Be sure to tell him about Pet Plants Day, and then I'll show you the drawings for the stage set we're going to build to put your giant plants on for the open house—with spotlights, too!"

Michael hurried into the outer office and called home. But the voice that answered was not Norman. It was Mom.

Chapter 17

Michael almost dropped the phone.

"Where are you?" she asked. "I just walked in the door, and you're supposed to be here. I was worried."

"But you don't get home on Wednesdays until six."

"You're still supposed to be here. I got off work early today because a reporter called this morning about coming over after school with a photographer. They'll be here in twenty minutes. Now why aren't you here?"

A reporter and photographer! Michael started to panic. "Mom, I really need to talk to Norman for a minute. Quick! Then I can explain."

"No, explain first."

He told her about Pet Plants Day. "Now can I talk to Norman? It's important!"

"Awards?" said Mom.

"For you and Dad, too," said Michael. "For being such great parents to let us have such big pet plants. Now I need to talk to Norman."

"The little plants will be bigger by next fall, so that should work out fine," said Mom.

"But that won't work. The principal is counting on the giant ones being even bigger by then. He's going to send a truck and put them on a stage with spotlights and everything! We can't show up with some teensy little things. Everybody's already seen Stanley and Fluffy at the science fair and on TV. They'd know that smaller ones are fakes. We have to bring the real ones that started the pet plant movement. Would you put Norman on the phone, please?"

"Then I guess we may have to reconsider," said Mom. "Your father and I were discussing this whole mess again after you left for school this morning. Norman is so attached to Fluffy, and you've done such an outstanding job of changing your messy ways. Besides, we're absolutely stuck on how to get rid of the big plants, and the cuttings are just not growing. Maybe we can find another way to work out the vacation problem."

"Great, Mom! Thanks! Now I have to talk to Norman."

"Quick," he told Norman, "tell Jason and Bob we're calling off the junkathon. I think the plants are saved, so we don't have to do it."

Norman whispered, "But we already did. You're going to love it. It's the biggest mess I ever saw."

"No! This will wreck everything! Keep Mom busy in the kitchen, and get Jason and Bob to sneak all the junk back out of the house."

"I can't. They took off as soon as we got done," Norman whispered. "They didn't want to be around when Mom and Dad found out what we did."

"But a reporter and photographer are coming!" said Michael. "Tell Mom nobody can go in our room until I get there because I have to clean up a few things."

"I'll try," promised Norman.

Michael told Mr. Leedy he had to go and ran most of the way home.

Mom and Norman were sitting in the living room talking to a man who was taking notes and a woman holding a camera. Michael hurried by, saying, "Don't come in our room yet. I just have to pick up a few things."

"Hurry up," said Mom.

Michael went in and closed the door. The guys had done a great job. He was surrounded by junk. In some places it was piled as high as his chin. There was no time to think. He had to do something—anything—fast.

Climbing over the heaps to the closet door, he forced it open and shoved as much stuff as possible in as quickly as he could. Then he pushed hard against the door to force it shut.

There was no way to carry the rest out without Mom seeing, even if there had been time. Frantic, Michael realized there was only one thing to do.

He climbed over piles to the window, struggled to open it, and started pitching junk out onto the lawn. They would have to lug it all back to Mrs. Smith's garage later.

Most of the big things went out the window easily. The bottom layer turned out to be mostly Michael's own junk, scattered from the boxes that had been in the closet. Strewn all over the floor, there were too many little things to pick up in a hurry. So he grabbed Mrs. Smith's snow shovel.

Starting in the middle of the room, he shoveled half the stuff under his bed and the other half under Norman's.

He heard Mom's voice in the hall and getting closer. He shut the window and pulled the curtains across to hide the heaps outside. Just in time! He heaved a sigh of relief.

Then he realized he still had the snow shovel. He grabbed his bedspread and wrapped it around the handle. From the drawer where Norman kept his best things, he pulled out the gorilla head and put it over the handle. He topped that with Norman's baseball cap.

Opening the door, Mom saw the usual neat room but with the curtains closed. Michael and a short gorilla wearing a bedspread and baseball cap leaned casually against the wall.

"Who's in there?" Mom asked the gorilla.

"Nobody," said Michael.

"Thank goodness," said Mom. "Open the curtains so we'll have more light for the pictures."

"Never mind," said the photographer. "My lighting equipment is enough. The curtains will make a nice neutral background to show off the plants. They certainly are big!"

Norman was looking around, amazed. He whispered close to Michael's ear, "Where did you put it?"

"Mostly out the window," Michael whispered back.

Norman stood up straight and smiled winningly for the camera. "Say cheese, Fluffy," he said.

"Don't even joke about that," warned Mom.

"Let's get another shot with some kind of action," said the photographer. "Could you get a pitcher and be watering them?"

"I've got something better," said Norman. Before Michael could do anything but say "Don't," Norman grabbed the closet door knob and yanked.

Junk toppled out all over him.

They all helped dig him out.

"You said the window," Norman snarled at Michael.

"What about the window?" asked Mom.

"Nothing important," said Michael.

Mom took a closer look at the junk. "What is all this stuff?"

She tossed aside a dented tea kettle, four pairs of high-heeled shoes, and a bicycle seat. Picking up some magazines and books, she read the titles aloud. "Twenty-year-old *True Romance* magazines? *Favorite Egg Recipes? Knit Your Way to Fun and Profit? How to Get Your Kids to Do What You Want?*" She tucked that one under her arm.

"And these things all have price stickers on them! I shudder to think what the answer to this question will be, but I have to ask it. Are you holding a garage sale in this closet?"

"Not exactly," said Michael.

"Open the curtains," commanded Mom, "so we can get a better look at this stuff."

"That's not a good idea," said Michael.

The photographer, who was standing near the window, pushed the curtains aside, revealing a scenic view of the junk heaps outside.

"Perhaps there is a logical explanation for all this," said Mom grimly. "But in the meantime, consider yourself grounded for the rest of your life!"

"That's too long," protested Michael.

"We'll discuss this later."

The reporter was looking through the books on the floor. "I'll take these two," he said, handing Norman two quarters.

"I can use this bicycle seat," said the photographer. "And that brown purse would be good with my new suit." Norman handed them to her, and she handed him four dollars.

"Anything else?" he asked helpfully. "A tea kettle? A purple lampshade? Three empty coffee cans?"

"I could use the coffee cans," she said. "They're great for keeping little junk in."

"Do you want to buy some little junk to put in

them?'' asked Michael. ''We got a good selection under the beds.''

''How much do you want for this camera?'' asked the reporter. ''There's no price tag on it.''

''That's MY camera,'' said the photographer, snatching it away from him. She went outside to look through the pile on the lawn.

Mom turned to the reporter. ''I know you'll understand that I'm not trying to conceal anything here—how could I? But I have to ask if you would leave this mess out of the story you're going to write. It doesn't have anything to do with pet plants.''

''I do understand,'' he replied. ''My kids are messy, too. Pet plants are news. Messy kids are not.''

By the time the reporter and photographer left, the junk supply had gone down considerably, and Norman was holding almost thirty dollars.

''I guess I have to give this to Mrs. Smith,'' he said wistfully.

''Why?'' asked Mom, who was lying on Michael's bed reading *How to Get Your Kids to Do What You Want.*

''This is mostly her garage sale,'' explained Michael. ''We borrowed it.''

''How did you get her to let you do that?''

''Norman talked her into it. She thinks he's cute.''

''This is not my fault,'' squawked Norman. ''It was Michael's idea.''

Michael explained why they had borrowed Mrs. Smith's garage sale and how he had tried to call it off, but everything had gone wrong anyway. He also said he was sorry.

''Actually,'' said Mom, ''this was very resourceful of you. I'm amazed.''

''You're not upset any more?''

"According to this book, I have nothing to be upset about. I'm not the one who has to clean all this up."

"Uh-oh," said Norman.

"Right," said Mom. "I'm just going to relax and read my new book while you two do all the work."

"You owe twenty-five cents for the book," said Norman.

"Get it out of my purse. Then after you finish carrying Mrs. Smith's garage sale back to her garage, you can both cook dinner."

"But all I know how to cook good is popcorn," said Norman. "Michael could make fudge ripple pancakes."

"You know how to make hamburgers and vegetables, and how to open cans. Here's a simple little recipe for stewed prunes in this book."

"Yuk," said Michael. "I'd rather eat stewed socks!"

"Be careful what you wish for," said Mom. "That could be arranged."

"She IS still upset," grumbled Norman.

Mom grinned. "I'll feel a lot better after I finish reading this book. Now get going!"

The boys were trudging across the lawn with their loads of junk when Dad drove in. They started from the beginning to explain all over again.

Dad took it calmly. "I'm too tired to get upset," he said. "All I want to do is relax and eat dinner. Do you know what we're having?"

"Norman and I are cooking," said Michael. "Probably popcorn and stewed prunes."

Now Dad looked upset. He stomped off into the house, calling for Mom.

After the last of many trips to Mrs. Smith's garage, the boys found their parents in the kitchen eating heated-up frozen dinners. "Yours are in the oven," said Mom. "Your father changed my mind about you two cooking tonight."

"Since going away on vacation is out for this year," said Dad, "we've been talking about some one-day trips we could take so at least we'll be going somewhere."

"Surely we can figure out how to get rid of the plants by vacation time next year," said Mom soothingly.

"Maybe there's a way we could still go to Disney World this year," said Michael. He figured it was worth a try. "We could rent a limo from Jason's uncle to drive Fluffy and Stanley along on vacation while we go in our car."

"NO!" said Mom and Dad.

"A moving van?"

"No," they said.

"A camper!"

"The plants are too tall for a camper," said Mom.

"We can get one with a sunroof that opens so they can stick out," said Michael.

Dad stopped chewing his dinner and looked thoughtful. "Well, it would be weird," he said, "but it would be better than not going at all."

Michael held his breath and waited for Mom to stop chewing.

"Hmm," she said, "that might even save some money because even though we'd have to rent the camper, we wouldn't have to pay for motels and restaurant meals."

"Yay!" yelled Norman.

"But," added Mom.

"What?" asked Michael, Norman, and Dad together.

"What if it rains? With the sunroof open, the inside of the camper will get soaked, and so will we."

"We can all wear our raincoats in the camper," said Norman.

"Plastic," said Michael desperately. "A really big piece of plastic! We can tie it over the plants. Or tape it down. Or something. We'll figure it out somehow."

"I'll bring my umbrella," added Norman.

"Maybe it won't rain," muttered Dad.

"Well," said Mom, "I really do want to go to Disney World."

"Yay!" yelled Norman. He ran off to tell Fluffy.

Mom got paper and pencil to figure out how many socks they would need for the trip.

When no one was looking, Michael sneakily poured some cough syrup on the cuttings.

Dad started looking through the phone book for camper rental companies.

The boys were so happy and tired that they both fell asleep as soon as they crawled into bed. They slept soundly through the plants' dinner and burps and Fluffy's usual "Ex."

One of Stanley's vines rested gently on Michael's shoulder as he dreamed about the plants starring in the spotlights on the school stage. Everybody in the whole school and Mom and Dad were singing along off-key with Norman, "Doo-dah-doo-dah."

Michael woke up. He could still hear "Doo-dah" very loud and off-key, but Norman's eyes were closed and his mouth was not moving. Could he possibly have learned ventriloquism? Not likely.

"Shut up, Fluffy," said Michael. He patted Stanley's vine and went back to sleep. He had not noticed yet the hundreds of little green buds that had sprouted all over Stanley during the night—the tiny beginnings of sock-shaped seed pods.